Z. O. Anderson, brings you a new Suspenseful and Entertaining" Journey that is filled with characters and events that represents everyday situations, accept this group of people has a time travel device and the option to travel back in time to prevent events from happening.

As this team of time travelers makes their way to the past, so they can travel back to the future to prevent several deaths of their loved ones. Anderson "keeps the reader guessing what will happen next."

By Michael J. Kiser
Author of
The End Times – What Is It Really About?

SOUTH
STAR

Z.O. Anderson

DragonEye Publishing

SOUTH STAR

5

To JACKIE

"A South Star is a Nova. A Nova is a star that suddenly increases greatly in brightness, then within a few years, or a few months, grows dim again. A South Star is also a person who only gets fifteen minutes of fame. Or like a Rock Group or Singer with a single hit, or a One-Hit-Wonder. South Star is also used to describe the short-lived Confederacy of the 1860's."

--Frank Zachary

PROLOGUE

They all met while they were attending college at the University of Colorado in Boulder. They became better acquainted at their favorite watering hole, that tavern across from their favorite gambling casino.

It was in the tavern that they began to discuss their time travel theories and plans. Of course, the drunker they became, the more ingenious, and oft times absurd, their fabulous ideas became.

Eventually, they acquired funding for their experiments and their Time Travel Project. But, when they were finally successful, the government moved in and took control. Even so, they still managed to do things their own way.

SOUTH
STAR

"We can record the animals in the valley from that sun dial rock at the edge of the plateau." Frank explains to the others.

The Cameraman, Bill Clark, filming with video cameras in both hands, follows Frank. The Monitor, Steve Johnson, carrying recording equipment, checks his chronometer and yells out alarmed:

"Frank! We traveled too far back in time. It should be five million years B.C. This is more like fifty million years B.C."

Team leader Frank Zachary, in his early forties, seeming much huskier in new khaki coveralls than his usual wiry appearance, checks his own chronometer.

"Yeah, yeah. It's that negative accelerator...I can fix that." He shrugs his shoulders then tells them, "Let's take a look anyway."

The three men, all dressed in coveralls and loaded down with scientific equipment, move cautiously
toward the sun dial-shaped rock at the edge of the plateau.

That was how they had arrived, all geared down, in a clearing on this prehistoric plateau, exiting from a silky gossamer-like spiraling vertical vortex that suddenly materialized out of nowhere. They had stepped out of this portal and looked around in awe. The animals, birds and other prehistoric life forms were gargantuan. This very calm, clear and peaceful day was disrupted only by the strange and unusual sounds emanating from the valley below which was overgrown with gigantic vegetation and blanketed with an eerie mist.

Cameraman Bill Clark, filming a large bird circling ominously above them, shouts out, "Frank, look out! That giant bird is diving at you!"

Frank drops to the ground, puts a whistle in his mouth and blows hard. The shrill whistle startles the huge bird and makes it veer off.

Then Monitor Steve Johnson alerts Cameraman Bill Clark, "Look out, yourself! There's a small Raptor right behind you."

The Raptor charges Cameraman Clark, who screams and runs away.

Frank cries out to him. "Don't run! It's only a baby raptor. Blow your whistle and scare it off, or use your stun gun."

Bill tries to blow the whistle as he runs, but he trips and falls. Then he starts kicking at the little raptor. The raptor chomps down on Bill's leg and lifts him up in the air.

Frank blows his whistle and throws rocks at the raptor. One rock hits the raptor on the nose and it lets out a roar, opening its mouth and dropping the Cameraman. Then the raptor quickly turns to face Frank. Frank charges, waving his arms and yelling as the little raptor backs away. Frank stops and whistles again. The raptor eyes him cautiously then begins to circle him. Frank circles with it until he's between the raptor and Cameraman Clark. Steve Johnson moves over to help Bill as Frank keeps the young raptor at bay.

"Oh, oh! Here comes the Momma!" Steve yells as he points past the small raptor.

A much larger raptor comes running and roaring toward them.

"Activate the wormhole! Frank commands. "Hurry!"

Monitor Steve Johnson pulls out a remote device and clicks it. That silky gossamer-like spiraling vertical vortex re-appears behind them.

Frank and Steve pick up the Cameraman Clark and run for the vortex. The three men disappear into the wormhole just as the large raptor charges at them.

Frank, Steve and Bill come flying out of the wormhole into a laboratory and land on a platform surrounded by huge humming accelerators.

"Shut it down!" Frank commands the Technicians. "Quick, shut it down!"

Head Technician Stephanie Andrea Valerie immediately throws emergency switches and the wormhole begins to fade just as the big Raptor sticks its head into the laboratory. As the wormhole disappears, the big Raptor disappears with it.

A large wall calendar in the background reads, "**May 2000**".

"Medic!" yells Frank. " We have a medical emergency!"

The squirming Cameraman Clark holds his leg as the Medics come charging over and begin cleaning and dressing his wounds. They bring a stretcher and as they start to carry him out, he grabs Frank by the arm and says, "It looks like you'll need a new Cameraman, Frank."

"He'll need a new Monitor, too... I <u>quit!</u>" Steve Johnson exclaims as he hands his equipment to a lab assistant and heads for the exit.

Frank chases after him. "Wait! Wait!"

Steve Johnson exits the building almost at a run with Frank right on his heels.

This modern scientific laboratory building made of steel and glass glistens in the sunlight as men and women dressed in white laboratory coats stroll in and out of the entrances.

A sign in front reads: "PROJECT TX-7, WATERTON CANYON, COLORADO."

Frank grabs Johnson by the arm and spins him around. "Listen! Don't you dare tell those people at the Synergist Syndicate about this space-time mix-up. Do you hear me!" Frank warns.

Johnson says nothing. He just turns and walks away.

Frank turns around and heads back to the building. As he starts to re-enter the building, his daughter Patricia, a lovely sweet-sixteen, wearing a jogging suit and carrying a gym bag, bounds out the door.

"Hi, daddy!" she chirps as she throws her arms around his neck and gives him a big hug and a kiss. He hugs and kisses her in return.

"Patty, what are you doing here?" he asks.

"I came to see Momma and Auntie Audra about that Synergist party. Mom is a guest speaker and she said I could go if my karate instructor, Samurai Sam, accompanies me." She tells him.

Frank slaps his forehead as he exclaims, "Patty, that's not a party. It's a protest rally and they are protesting against us!

Patty argues, "I don't understand why. The Synergist Syndicate was such a big part of this project. Auntie Audra dearly loved them for putting up all that money."

"Aw, sweetie" Frank explains, "The government cancelled their TX-7 Monitor contract, so now they're protesting against us to try and get it back."

"I still want to go. Nathan Janelle is going to be there!" Patty squeals excitedly as she jumps up and down clapping her hands.

"Nathan the Rock Star!" Frank feigns being shocked. "We're doomed!"

"Daddy, quit being silly." She chides him. "Nathan is so gorgeous! His music is so fantastic! He always gets involved in political causes and he's talked with the President and the Pope...and he's so gorgeous!"

Frank checks his wristwatch with the facility clock tower. "It's time for your karate class, princess."

"I'm on my way, bye!" Patty skips down the street.

Frank looks after her lovingly then turns to enter the building and bumps into someone in a white laboratory coat. Papers fly everywhere.

The box containing the papers reads: "SYNERGIST SYNDICATE."

Frank slaps his forehead again.

In Littleton, Colorado, the twenty-story, white granite-faced building contrasts sharply with the less pretentious structures of this Rocky Mountain seat of power and money. All the other buildings in this luxurious office complex are dark brown in color.

A very tasteful sign over the entrance reads: "SYNERGIST SYNDICATE."

Another tasteful sign below that reads: "HOME OF NUTRIONICS."

Inside, caterers dressed in white jackets busily put the finishing touches on several tables that are lavishly adorned with a variety of luscious foods and beverages. One table, centrally located, displays a variety of Nutrionics products. Over this table is an elaborate sign reading, "Nutrionics — Our New Fountain Of Youth".

Ryan Terrance Michaels, a stately looking man in his early-forties, impeccably dressed in an Armani business suit, enters and goes directly to the center table to check the Nutrionics displays.

Frank Zachary and Ryan ("Rye") Michaels had been college roommates at the University of Colorado in Boulder. Frank and Rye were the best of friends at one time. Since Frank was such a hothead and Rye was cool, calm and collected, they were known as "Frank and Sense" around the campus. Rye Michaels was the "Star from the South". Frank was the cowboy.

Satisfied with the Nutrionics display, Michaels turns and addresses the caterers with a very charming and mellow Southern accent, "Caterers! If y'all please..."

The caterers stop what they're doing and gather around him.

He continues, "There will be celebrities as well as political figures here today, along with our regular supporters. Please, keep the champagne glasses filled at all times." He pauses and moves toward the food and beverage tables with the caterers following him.

"Also, we're having a guest speaker from Project TX-7. Do not allow anyone to harass her. We have our own professional interview team who will ask her very specific questions to elicit the information we need. Should anyone else try to butt in, quickly fill their glass, or offer them something else."

The caterers all nod to show they understand. Two of the caterers, gruff-looking men with unbuttoned jackets, appear suspiciously out-of-place. Rye glares at them. They quickly button up their jackets and try to look busy.

A white-haired ex-Senator comes in and makes a fuss. "Rye Michaels, we need to discuss this little shindig of yours!" former Senator Nick Genna harangues. Senator Genna, after his term in the Senate, started lobbying for the Synergist Syndicate, was hired by them and then gained a seat on their Board of Directors.

Rye stops him abruptly. "Please, Senator, I'm giving these caterers last minute instructions before our guests begin arriving."

Senator Genna won't be put off. "As a member of the Synergist Board of Directors, it is my job to keep an eye on this protest rally crap you're trying to pull. You don't know what's at stake here."

"I know perfectly well what's at stake." Rye replies curtly. "We are trying to get our contract with Project TX-7 re-instated." Rye picks up and examines a Nutrionic sample as he continues, "And if I'm successful, I'll be joining you on that Board Of Directors because of a very generous stock option."

Senator Genna continues to object. "Well, I don't think throwing a protest rally will work. In fact, it could screw up everything. Our plan is..."

Rye cuts him off. "I know the plan, Senator. I was a TX-7 Monitor before the government terminated our contract."

Frank Zachary's Monitor, Steve Johnson, from TX-7 pokes his head in the door, motions to Rye then ducts back out. Rye quickly brushes off the Senator.

"Senator, please, one of my informants has just arrived. This is very important.

"Very well." The Senator backs off, but as he starts to leave, "Let me say this.. If this little scheme of yours fails, your ass is mine!"

Senator Genna walks out leaving Rye to ponder his fate if his plan fails, but Rye just sneers at the exiting Senator. Then Rye quickly goes to meet with Steve Johnson.

Johnson enters and explains in a lowered voice what happened at TX-7. "...And then I told them I quit..." he says.

Rye goes ballistic when he hears this. "No! Don't quit! I need you there!"

Johnson tries to object, "But, I thought I'd come here..."

Rye cuts him off. "No! Go back! I need to know everything... everything that they are doing at all times. Now go back there and pick up where you left off."

Johnson shrugs his shoulders, nods his head and leaves.

In the lobby of the TX-7 Research Facility, Frank Zachary, now wearing a suit and tie, stares at the ticking second hand of a large clock on the wall. He synchronizes his wristwatch with the clock.

Audra Ashley, a smartly dressed, bright and chipper forty-something, approaches. Frank begins to squirm and looks for a way out, but Audra catches him.

"Frank! Roger is waiting for us."

He hesitates and protests. "Audra. I can't stand those people."

"Oh, please. We're counting on you." She insists.

Frank relents and follows her through a door marked "Laboratory".

The brightly lit, spotlessly clean scientific laboratory buzzes with activity as technicians dressed in white lab coats scurry about checking instruments and equipment.

Roger Dane, distinguished looking in his late-fifties, checks his pocket watch with the wall clock. He sees Audra and Frank enter and turns to a group of Government Observers.

"Ladies and Gentlemen, we are ready now. I'm Doctor Roger Adam Dane, Director of Time Travel Project TX-7."

Frank and Audra approach, but Frank reluctantly lags behind.

Roger introduces them. "This is Doctor Audra Heather Ashley, our quantum physicist. Doctor Ashley is actually the brains behind this entire project."

Audra smiles and cordially nods at everyone. Roger then turns to Frank. "And this is our Chief Engineer, Franklin Zachary."

Frank waves slightly like he's flipping them the bird. His smile is more like a sneer as he defiantly folds his arms in front of himself to indicate that he's not going to cooperate.

The Head Observer steps forward. "They tell us you're traveling back to prehistoric time to try to determine the origin of our species." He observes.

Audra immediately responds, "Yes, we're going back four and a half million years when man was beginning to evolve..."

An arrogant young Observer asks, "Just how does one review four and one half million years to make such a determination?"

Audra responds politely, "We go back to prehistory and mark the date and time. Then we travel back and forth in stages to record events that will hopefully tell us the prehistoric period of man's evolution. Yes, it may take some time to complete, but then..."

Roger Dane quickly interjects, "...But then if we are successful, we'll begin a search for `The Missing Link'."

The arrogant young Observer responds sarcastically. "How nice."

Roger immediately moves to the central platform and everyone follows him.

"They tell us you time travel by wormhole." The Head Observer queries.

Roger turns and puts his hand on Frank's shoulder and tells the Observer, "Our Chief Engineer, Frank Zachary, will explain all our procedures for you."

Frank hesitates. He looks pleadingly at Audra. She looks away. He sighs then advances up to the front. He points to the large cylinders that surround the central platform and speaks rapidly in order to finish quickly. The faster he can get through this, the better.

"Those large circular accelerators, when activated, create a vortex, or wormhole." Then Frank points to a smaller cylinder overhead and speaks even faster. "Then we give it a negative charge from the small accelerator up top in order to stabilize it."

They all look up and move in for a closer look.

In order to slow Frank down, Audra immediately intervenes.

"The position of the small accelerator is very important... Actually, It's extremely <u>critical</u>." She emphasizes.

The arrogant young Observer lashes out sarcastically. "Ryan Terrence Michaels, of the Synergist Syndicate, says that solar flare activity interferes with the stabilization process and makes a stable wormhole impossible."

Roger looks apprehensively at Audra. She responds hesitantly.

"A stable wormhole is not impossible during solar flare activity... Just a little more difficult." She tries to reassure them.

The arrogant young Observer starts in again, "Ryan Terrence Michaels claims that if the Synergist Syndicate still had charge of your Monitors..."

Frank cuts him off, "Synergist lost their contract because they tried to use it for profit and to gain control of the Nutrionics market"

A female Observer quickly intercedes to everyone's relief:

"Doctor Ashley, tell us about these Monitors he just mentioned. What do they do? What equipment do they use?" She asks.

"Please follow me!" Audra says as she heads toward a door marked 'Equipment Room'. Everyone follows her in and she leads them to a table where they have displayed a variety of scientific equipment and other items. Audra loves to explain these things and she gushes out with much enthusiasm:

"Each Monitor maintains a personal journal that they keep with them at all times, in case a paradox is created and no one remembers anything." She explains to them.

Audra picks up a History book that she always keeps on hand and waves it around.

Then she continues, "They maintain a history data bank in their computers. We must closely review Monitor recordings after each trip to make absolutely certain that nothing has changed."

She moves to a small attaché case and opens it. "Here we have the Monitor's equipment, which consists of a laptop computer with a camcorder that can be attached to playback any recordings." She continues as she shows them a small recorder with a microphone headset. "They can also record vocally with this recorder."

They all gather around and examine the equipment, apparel and other items.

Audra continues, "The Monitors closely record all the activities of each member of the time travel team, including themselves."

The Head Observer comments, "You mentioned `Paradox'. A paradox is a statement that seems contrary to common sense and yet is perhaps true."

Audra responds, "Yes, but this type of paradox is a change in the course of historical events caused by a time traveler altering something in the past... For example, if you cause the death of one of your own grandparents while traveling in the past, you may cancel yourself out and cease to exist. This is the type of paradox to which we often refer." She explains.

Everyone becomes a little squeamish at such a thought. Some shiver and rub their arms like this thought gives them the chills. What a prospect!

The female Observer quickly changes the subject.

"What does the Cameraman do, Doctor Ashley?" She asks.

Audra moves to a different display of video recorders and begins to explain. "The Cameraman records the surrounding areas, such as the scenery, the life forms, prehistoric or otherwise, like the animals, birds..."

The arrogant young Observer cuts in jokingly, "The birds and the bees and the flowers and the trees..."

Frank becomes irate. "Oh knock it off! Why don't you go join Rye Michaels and his other flunkies at that Synergist protest rally."

Audra intercedes to calm Frank down. "Frank, please! I'm sure Synergist is only trying to help us."

Frank snaps back, "Bull! They're trying to shut us down until they can get their contracts back."

In the banquet room of the Synergist Syndicate building, semi-formally attired men and women surround the tables of food and beverages, helping themselves and chatting away.

Patty Zachary is with Rock Star Nathan at one of the tables, getting his autograph on a dozen different items. Her karate instructor, Samurai Sam, talks to Nathan's bodyguard. Nathan's bodyguard keeps putting his hand out occasionally to restrain Patty from Nathan.

Rye Michaels steps forward, raises his champagne – filled glass and addresses the guests, "Ladies and Gentlemen, if y'all please, a toast..."

The guests turn and raise their champagne glasses.

Rye continues, "To success in our quest to close down Project TX-7 until there are much tighter controls over said project."

`Hear! Hear!" resounds throughout the room.

Everyone drinks. Rye puts down his glass and everyone prepares themselves for one of his elaborate speeches:

"As you all know, we were among the first supporters to finance the TX-7 experiments. We were in charge of the Monitors, who scrutinized their every move and we fully intend to regain that important responsibility. I thank each and every one of you for coming."

Everyone applauds and the Senator Nick Genna comes over to Rye. "Arriana Zachary of TX-7 is an hour late. You say she's the Project Coordinator."

Rye tells him, "Yes, and she'll tell us much about Project TX-7's progress, whether she realizes it or not. So, please be patient, Senator."

But the Senator is not. "I don't have time to be patient. If she doesn't show up soon, I'm leaving...and just keep in mind what I said."

Rye responds with sarcasm, "I thank you for your confidence and support... Senator."

Arriana Zachary, thirty-something, attractive and elegantly dressed, enters and quickly walks toward Rye. Following her is a hulk of a man who keeps looking around as though he's suspicious of everyone.

"I don't see Patty or her escort, Rye." Arriana says to him as she looks around.

Rye makes a big fuss. "Arriana Dawnna Zachary! My word! We've all been beside ourselves wondering what happened to y'all."

Arriana explains, "I would have been here much sooner, but this klutz of a bodyguard they sent... I did not order any bodyguard. He insists that the Project hired him for me."

They all turn and look at the big burly man in his late-thirties who came in with her. He gruffly introduces himself.

"I'm Walt Marcson. TX-7 sent me to guard her, 'cuz they don't trust none of you people at this here protest meeting."

Arriana raises her hands in disgust. The Senator frowns. Rye taps Arriana on the arm and points to the table where Patty and Samurai Sam are with Nathan.

"Your daughter, Patricia, is at that table with Rock Star, Nathan Janelle."

Then Rye turns to Marcson, "And Mister Walt Marcson, I'd like to speak with you outside for a minute and discuss your attitude."

Walt shrugs his shoulders and follows Rye. Walt looks back at Arriana, taps his wristwatch and holds up one finger indicating that he'll be right back.

She looks disgusted and replies loudly, "Take your time. Better yet, stay away." Arriana goes to the table with Patty and Nathan.

In the hallway outside the banquet room, Rye leads Walt down the hall and makes certain that they are alone.

"Walt, you're overdoing it!" Rye chides him.

"Hey, you told me to make it look good." Marcson replies.

"Don't get carried away!" Rye harshly reprimands him.

"Okay, okay. I'll tone it down. Take it easy." Walt checks his wristwatch with the clock on the wall. "You've got less than fifteen minutes to get out of here." He tells Rye.

Rye ponders for a moment then looks back at the banquet room.

"No. I'm going back. I'm concerned about Arriana."
Walt protests. "That's my job, remember?"
Rye glares at him. Walt backs away shrugging his shoulders, Rye walks back to the banquet room with Walt following him.

Patty is eagerly showing her mother her memorabilia.
"Look at all the autograph's, Momma. I got each of my girlfriends some. They are all just simply going to die!" Patty exudes.
Arriana smiles. "Well, I'm glad you're having a good time. I'll be speaking soon, so tell Sam that I'll need all the support I can get from both of you."
"Okay." Patty tells her. "We'll be cheering you on all the way...0h, I told Nathan all about how Daddy and Rye Michaels were always fighting over you until Daddy won."
Arriana rolls her eyes then starts back toward Rye. Patty rejoins Sam.
SUDDENLY...several masked men in camouflage uniforms charge in and start shooting at the guests. Everyone dives for cover. The two caterers Rye reprimanded earlier pull out weapons and join the attackers.
Rye and Walt rush over and shove Arriana under a table. Sam and Nathan's bodyguard push Patty and Nathan under another table.
The Aggressors selectively shoot some guests and just hit or beat up others. Sam and Nathan's bodyguard start to fight back, but the attackers shoot them both down then grab Patty and Nathan.
Senator Genna yells out. "Look! They're abducting Nathan and the girl."

Walt Marcson pulls out a pistol, shoots and kills the Senator. Rye grabs Marcson. They struggle over the gun. The gun goes off and hits Rye in the soft part of his shoulder (prearranged, of course), and Rye falls back. Marcson then quickly disappears out a side door.

When the Aggressors grab Patty and Nathan, Patty fights back, trying to help Nathan. She kicks her abductor in the groin then starts using her karate to beat them away from herself and Nathan. One of the caterers turns and shoots Patty.

Arriana screams and runs to Patty as the attackers kidnap Nathan and make their escape. They disappear as quickly as them came.

Rye Michaels, holding his wounded shoulder, runs to Arriana, who is holding a bloody Patty in her arms.
"Get a doctor! Somebody call an ambulance!" Rye yells.

At the hospital emergency room, Frank comes running in and hurriedly approaches the duty Nurse. "My wife and daughter ... Arriana and Patricia Zachary..."
"Yes sir." The Nurse responds. "Patricia Erin Zachary was taken to surgery."
Frank starts toward the sign marked "Surgery" but the Nurse calls to him.
"But Mrs. Arriana Dawnna Zachary is just down the hall in a stall."
Frank stops, looks undecided for a moment them hurries down the hall to Arriana.
Frank is holding Arriana's hand when Rye Michaels, shoulder bandaged and arm in a sling, comes by and stops at the door. He stares at Arri and then at Frank and says, "They took out all our Security Guards, Frank.

They knew exactly what they were doing...Don't worry, we're going to get them." Rye tries to reassure him.

Rye knows that your best defense is a good offense, so he's telling Frank that he is now on the offensive and will actively do everything he can to track down the offenders. He is trying his best to be convincing, so that Frank will believe that Rye was just as much a victim as the others. But, does Frank really believe him?

Frank is pacing back and forth in the Surgery waiting room when Audra and Roger Dane come in.

"Arriana is in the Emergency Room." Frank tells them. "She's still in shock, sedated. Patty is still in surgery."

Roger tells him. "Our Security is investigating very thoroughly, Synergist claims that the attackers were working for TX-7. That's absolutely preposterous!"

Audra adds, "The attackers are demanding ransom for young Rock Star, Nathan Janelle." The Surgeon enters, takes off his mask and shakes his head negatively.

Frank drops to his knees, the emotions flooding his mind, pain too unbearable he feels his heart will break.

Audra sobs uncontrollably. Dane puts his arms around Audra to console her.

Later that day, at the TX-7 Laboratory, Roger Dane addresses the technicians and staff members.

"Synergist is blaming TX-7 agents for the attack on their protest rally and the abduction of Nathan Janelle. This project is being put on hold until a full investigation has been completed. Doctor Audra and

Frank are still at the hospital with Arriana. Patty's funeral arrangements are being made..." He chokes up and stifles a sniffle then takes a deep breath. "We may be shut down for as long as six months. You'll all be notified when we're ready to start up again."

They all moan and grumble as they head for the exits.

In church, Patty's body lays in state at the front of the church with open casket. Frank stands beside her casket while Arriana and Audra sit in the first pew leaving space for him.

Frank thinks back. He remembers Patty's first steps. He remembers when he taught her how to swim… her first days in school. Tears fill his eyes and he turns away. The memories flood in and it's too much for him to bear. He looks back at Arriana and Audra. He stares at Audra, knowing that she will find a way so Frank can travel back and save his little girl. This thought calms him down as two men, dressed in dark suits, approach him.

In the first pew, Audra turns to Arriana and whispers. "I'm working on that special activator for Frank, so he can travel back and save Patty when..."

A very distraught Arriana nervously silences her. "Don't say anything here. Later!"

When the two men dressed in dark suits walk up to Frank, Audra grabs Arriana's arm.

"Those men talking to Frank look kind of suspicious. Have you ever seen them before?"

Arriana looks at them closely then becomes upset and starts wringing her hands.

"Oh dear! They look like some of Frank's old Navy SEAL buddies. I'm very worried about Frank." Arri says.

Audra raises her eyebrows because Arriana is more upset than Frank. She pats Arriana's hand. "There, there, dear. I'm more worried about you" she consoles.

When the service begins, Frank joins Arriana and Audra in the front pew.

At the cemetery, after Patty's burial, Frank goes to talk surreptitiously with a couple of official-looking men while Audra takes Arriana aside and with lowered voice confides in her. "I've almost completed the special activator that will allow Frank to take a side trip to prevent Patty's death. It will be six months before the project starts up again. Do you think Frank will be okay by then?" Audra asks.

Arriana is still distraught, but responds. "I don't know. Patty's death has torn him apart. I'm no better, myself." Then suddenly she decides. "Yes, let's do it!"

Audra cautions her, "You know that if the

Government finds out what we're doing, they will terminate all of us...and I don't mean fire us."

Arriana nods and they return to the limousines.

"Let's go back to the laboratory and I'll show you what I've done." Audra tells her.

When the two men leave, Frank walks over to another part of the Cemetery where another funeral is taking place... that of Samurai Sam. Sam's mother and brother are standing beside the grave. Frank feels guilty for this. He talked Sam into opening his karate studio in Denver. Sam was a Hollywood stuntman, putting on a show for the tourists in Los Angeles, California, when Frank first saw him.

"Hey, Samurai Sam! I know someone who will finance a part-time studio for you in Denver." Frank told him.

Sam liked the idea, and Patty and her friends and schoolmates started receiving very good self-defense lessons.

He turned back and watched as Audra and Arriana's limo drove away.

Frank already knows what Audra is going to do, but he has his own plans.

Monitor Steve Johnson (Rye Michael's spy) has returned to the TX-7 Laboratory. He adjusts his ID badge as he carries a recorder to the equipment room. As he passes through the laboratory, he sees Audra and Arriana working in an isolated area. Quietly he goes over and listens at the door. He sees the activator and from the surprised look on his face, he understands what they're talking about. He listens closely then moves quietly to the equipment room and puts away the recorder.

Johnson waits until it's clear. He cautiously moves to a side door, and then quickly exits.

At the Synergist Building, Rye Michaels sits behind his desk looking around the room at the Nutrionics displays all over the walls of his office. A large display of products adorns a table in the corner. He gets up and goes over to examine some of the products.

Walt Marcson enters by a back door, walks over and looks over Rye's shoulder.

"What is all this stuff, anyway?" asks Marcson.

Rye gives him the big pitch. "Nutrionics, they believe, are the life giving nutrients in the Earth's soil that were washed down into the crevices and caves of this planet as a result of Noah's flood, as detailed in the Bible. Before the Great Flood, Methuselah lived nine hundred years. His grandson, Noah, lived only seven hundred years and those after him lived even shorter lives. When these nutrients were discovered in the caves, the Synergist Syndicate began to process and distribute them as the 'New Fountain Of Youth'. People became healthier and began to live longer. We're making a fortune selling these products."

Rye returns to his desk, sits down then pushes an envelope toward Walt.

"Here's the money you'll need for South America." Rye practically barks at him.

Walt picks up the envelope and stuffs it into his jacket pocket.

"So you got your TX-7 contract back and paid the ransom for young Nathan." He says.

Rye snaps back at him, "There's much more to it than that, but we got what we wanted and I got what I wanted. Now get out of here!"

Walt heads for the back door. "If they time travel back and find out about us..."

Rye silences him, "Don't worry about it. I'll be there to keep an eye on everything. I'll make certain they don't find out."

"I met your Monitor spy Steve Johnson on his way out. He says Frank Zachary can make side trips with some new gadget."

Rye frowns at first when he hears that Walt knows about it, but then he smiles slyly. "I'll be watching Frank like a hawk. I can assure y'all that he'll never get a chance to use it."

"Why don't you just kill him?" Walt asks. He looks at a photograph on the wall behind Rye. It's a photo of Rye and Frank in Navy uniforms below a Navy SEAL emblem. They have their arms over each other's shoulders, both smiling like old Navy buddies.

Rye turns and looks at the photo and says, "One of these days I will kill him, but right now I need him... a lot more than I need you."

Walt gets very nervous at that remark and quickly exits waving, "Adios, Amigo!"

After Marcson leaves, Rye sits at his desk and covers his face with his hands wondering how things could have gone so wrong. He knows Frank will do everything in his power to use the Time Travel Project to go back and save Patty. What he must figure out now is how to back up Frank without exposing his part in the attack

and getting himself killed.

He wished Doctor Jackson Kaiden Ashley were still alive. Jack would know how to straighten things out. Jack Ashley, Audra's husband and love of her life, was the instigator of the Time Travel Project. Rye always called him Stonewall Jackson. Frank called him Jack and Audra always called him "Jackie". Jack was on his way to Washington D. C. to get Government financing for their Project when his plane crashed on take-off at Denver International Airport. Audra was totally crushed when her Jackie was killed. He and Frank promised they would help her time travel back to prevent Jack from boarding that fatal aircraft, but this was before the government moved in and took control. Then it became too dangerous for them to try anything.

Rye, Frank, Audra and Jackson all met at Colorado University in Boulder, Colorado, where they attended college. Jackson Ashley was always talking about time travel and everyone got to know each other much better at their favorite hangout ...the Nova Lounge.

The tavern in Blackhawk, Colorado, has a sign over it reading "NOVA LOUNGE". Above the sign is a star-shaped light that grows brighter and brighter, stays bright a minute, then gets dimmer and dimmer. It simulates the effects of a star that is going Nova.

Across the street, the large sign of the "SUPER NOVA CASINO" simulates an exploding star. Each time a customer hits a slot machine jackpot, the huge sign displays a colorful variety of exploding stars with cheers and noisy fireworks... an excellent attraction.

Frank Zachary sits at a table in a dark corner of the Nova Lounge. He appears to be extremely distraught with his hair disheveled and matted down and several days' growth of beard. He wears a black turtle-necked sweater, black slacks and a black jacket. Behind him on the wall is a pendulum clock. The clock face brightens and dims as the pendulum swings back and forth, just like the sign in front that simulates a star going Nova.

Frank slowly sips a drink as he spies on seven men sitting at tables near the back. The two caterers that joined the terrorists at the Synergist party are sitting with them, so he knows these are Patty's killers.

Soon, a man carrying a satchel enters and goes to their tables. He motions to the terrorists, points to the satchel and heads for the back door. They all get up and follow.

Frank sees them leaving, then he stands up and quickly exits by a side door.

In the alley behind the Nova Lounge, the eight men exit the back door and move down the alleyway. The man with the satchel opens it and pulls out bundles of money and waves it at them. They all smile and laugh then move to a more lighted up area under a street lamp.

The man with the satchel starts to pass out the money when suddenly Frank jumps out of the shadows and starts shooting them down with an automatic weapon.

Some pull out weapons and try to dive for cover, but Frank is too fast for them. All of them go down.

Frank tries unsuccessfully to question one or two that are still alive, but they know nothing other than the name "Marcson".

Frank then walks over and kicks the satchel. Money flies everywhere. The wind catches it and blows the money all over the area. Frank ignores the money and makes certain that all of the terrorists are dead. Then he disappears into the night.

It's six months later at the Project TX-7 Facility. Frank Zachary is once again waiting in the lobby. He looks much better now and is once again clean and dressed in khaki coveralls. He stares at the ticking second hand of the large clock on the wall, synchronizes his wristwatch with it and adjusts his ID badge.

The wall calendar reads, `**November 5th, 2000'**.

Audra Ashley comes rushing down the hall and motions to him.

"Frank! Come with me to my office. I have that special activator for you."

Frank immediately follows her. As they start down the hall, Roger Adam Dane comes out of the Laboratory and intercepts them.

"Audra! Those Government Observers are here again. They want to see more this time."

Audra and Frank stop and Audra tells Roger, "We'll run a test for them shortly.'

As she starts to walk away, Roger persists. "Some say that this is all smoke and mirrors. They want more proof. They want to step through the wormhole and see for themselves."

Audra turns to him with a smile on her face. "Good. We'll run Program TX-7g."

Roger looks stunned at first as he exclaims, "That prehistoric storm! We can't..." Then he pauses, "Oh, of course. Why didn't I think of that? We'll have that test ready to go in two hours."

Audra smiles again, "We'll be there."

She and Frank continue down the hall as Roger re-enters the Laboratory.

"I don't like that storm." Frank objects.

Audra assures him, "That prehistoric electrical storm will generate all the energy you'll need to maintain your second wormhole."

Frank smiles and follows her down the hall. "You've got this whole thing programmed."

Audra smiles back at him. "Exactly."

They enter Audra's office and she goes immediately to her wall safe. She removes the device and shows it to Frank. It resembles a TV remote control or small cell phone.

Arriana enters waving a dossier. "Audra, Security wants to know more about this new Cameraman you hired."

"Let me finish with Frank first then we'll discuss it." Audra tells her.

Arriana nods in agreement. Audra hands Frank the special activator and he examines it closely. She knows if this works, they'll be able to go back and save her Jackie, as well. She walks to a large map on the wall. Frank and Arriana follow her. Audra points to a marked spot on the map.

"You'll exit the second wormhole at these coordinates." She tells him.

"That's the alley behind the Synergist Building." Arriana adds.

Frank walks over and very closely studies the map. He tells them, "I've scrutinized all the investigative reports, and so I know exactly where each of those attackers will be, including the two caterers and that phony bodyguard of Arri's, Walt Marcson."

Audra explains, "The storm will pass in three hours. You must return from Synergist before the wormhole begins to deteriorate, or you will be trapped. And you know what will happen if you get trapped in the same time zone with yourself... or rather, your counterpart."

"I know." Frank responds. "I'll dissolve, or explode, or..."

Arriana gets very upset. "Never mind! Please! Take some extra medication for the Doppelganger effect. The closer you get to yourself, the weaker you'll become unless you take this medication to alter your metabolism so you'll have different brain wave vibrations than yourself, or your counterpart, or..."

Audra calms her down. "Arriana, please! Frank knows all that. He's been through things like this before."

Frank puts his arms around Arri to calm her down. Then, he kisses Arri, gives Audra a big hug, and slips the special activator into his pocket and exits.

Arriana picks up the dossier and opens it. "About this new Cameraman you hired."

"Tony Joshua." Audra responds. "He's a splendid Cameraman. He made Lauriena Sue Moreaux world famous."

Arriana rolls her eyes. "He's not filming any sexy movie stars on this prehistoric trip."

Audra adds, "He won a Pulitzer prize while he was working with the media."

Arriana exclaims, "He was working with the paparazzi!"

Suddenly Audra blurts out, "Samurai Sam was Tony's <u>brother</u>!"

Arriana looks stunned for a moment. "Does anyone else know about this?"

"No! Believe me, Arri, Tony is extremely well qualified for this job. He does excellent work. He comes highly recommended... and he can help Frank."

Arriana hands her the dossier and Audra immediately locks it in her wall safe.

Tony Joshua, twenty-five years old, handsome and self-assured, talks to the bartender at the Nova Lounge. The plush surroundings cater to a Yuppie crowd. The exception is an old drunk sitting next to Tony at the bar. The old drunk has a drink in front if him and he stares straight ahead almost in a catatonic state.

Tony explains to the bartender.

"I took their album photos. Songs like, 'How many buffalo did William Cody kill to gain the title of Buffalo Bill?' ... and..."

The bartender chuckles, "I don't know. How many?"

"One!" Tony responds. "One Old White Buffalo."

Everyone eyes Tony with disbelief.

The old drunk, staring straight ahead, butts in speaking in a slurred monotone-like voice.

"I read somewhere that Cody killed the old white buffalo using only his Bowie knife. Then he skinned it and gave the white robe to Chief Yellow Hand, whereupon the local natives gave Cody the noble and uncontested title of 'Buffalo Bill'."

Tony gets upset. "Hey, that's right! Thanks a lot, you old fart!"

The old drunk ignores Tony and just keeps rambling on, "That old white buffalo was ready to die anyway. It was the young white buffalo that stomped all over everybody, mainly Wild Bill Hickock. They made a movie out of that one, called `The White Buffalo', starring Charles Brons..."

Tony cuts him off, "Hey, just shut up!"

The old drunk returns to his catatonic state of staring straight ahead in silence.

The bartender corrects them. "History books say Cody killed over a hundred buffalo."

Tony smiles, "If you were a writer or historian and Wild Bill Hickock pointed a gun at your nose and said 'pick-a-number' what would you do?"

Then Tony leans over and talks confidentially to the bartender.

"I heard that the terrorists that shot up the Synergist Syndicate came over here and shot up this place, too."

"No, no! Not true!" The bartender replies emphatically. "They only met here to collect their money, but somebody killed all of them out back in the alley."

Tony hands him a business card.

"A great photo spread of the scene, with a good magazine article, could make you some big bucks, my man." Tony slyly eggs him on.

The bartender stares at Tony's card, ponders this for a while then smiles cunningly. "I think I might know somebody who just might know something about who killed them...uh... for a price, if you know what I mean."

Tony smiles and nods, "I know exactly what you mean... Hey, I've got a quick film shoot, but I'll be right back."

He gives the bartender the thumbs up sign and heads out the door.

At the TX-7 Laboratory, Roger Dane checks over three of the Government Observers who are now wearing light blue jump suits, so that they can step through the wormhole into a new time zone and check it out for themselves. The remaining Observers are still wearing their regular clothes.

Frank Zachary enters wearing new khaki coveralls and walks toward the Equipment Room. He tells Roger, "When my Monitor and that new Cameraman arrive, send them both into the equipment room."

Roger stops him. "Oh, by the way, the Synergist Syndicate is once again in charge of the Monitor Program, and they are sending over a new Monitor."

Frank is taken aback. "New Monitor? Who?"

Roger hesitantly responds. "Ryan Terrance Michaels."

Frank clenches his fists. The Arrogant Observer snickers and sneers. Frank glares at him, but suddenly Rye Michaels attracts everyone's attention as he enters boisterously, followed by Doctor Audra Ashley and the new Cameraman, Tony Joshua.

"That's me, if ya'll don't mind. I am the Monitor now, just like before, and I'm all ready to go." Rye takes a bow as everyone turns and looks at him then they applaud.

Frank moves forward and gets in his face. "Just remember that you're <u>only</u> the Monitor, Rye! I'm still in charge. You take orders from me. Got it!" Frank stares him in the eyes and Rye stares right back at him.

Then the corners of Rye's mouth lift in a sneer-like smile. "Just like old times. Right Frank?" Rye melodiously remarks.

Frank always was the Antagonist. Rye always managed to keep himself cool. On one summer job they had together at a manufacturing plant machine shop doing maintenance and cleanup work, Frank told the crew, "If a man's machine area is all dirty and cluttered, he looks around and says, `I'm working too hard, I'd better slow down'. But, if it's clean, he says, `It looks like I haven't been doing anything, I'd better hustle'... so, the cleaner we keep everything, the more everyone hustles."

This was Frank Zachary's `Philosophy Of Hustle'.

That worked well. It got them a raise and a bonus. Not bad for a summer job.

Frank is about to yell, but Roger interrupts their argument. "Please, gentlemen, let's not start that again. We've much to do. Ryan, I hope you remember everything from before."

"Yes, yes. I remember all of it. Let us proceed." Rye tells them.

Frank heads for the Equipment Room and everyone follows, including Roger, Audra, Rye, Tony and the Observers.

Rye goes immediately to the Monitor's equipment. Audra shows Tony his equipment.

Frank starts packing extra items. Rye notices this and quizzes him.

"I see you're packing a 'Boy Scout Kit'. Be Prepared, but why weapons, explosives and some lock-picking devices?" Rye knows what Frank plans to do, but he seeks a response.

Frank doesn't want Rye to know that it's for his side trip to rescue Patty, so he just makes up excuses. "Just old habits from our Navy SEAL days. You never know what kind of situations may arise if anything goes wrong."

Rye nods his head. That's a good explanation.

Tony balances a video camcorder on his shoulder and swaggers over to them. "Heyheyhey! I'm glad you guys know what to do, because this is my first trip."

Rye smiles and puts his arm around Tony's shoulder. "I'll bet y'all haven't heard the 'Butterfly Story'."

Tony gives him a side-glance. "No, but I'll bet y'all are gonna tell me about it."

Rye strikes a storytelling pose. "Why certainly...two million years ago, during the spring thaw in the Rocky

Mountains...Y'all have seen those signs 'Watch For Falling Rocks' ...A great tribal Chief was standing at the base of a mountain when a small girl chasing a butterfly bumped into him. He laughed, picked up the child and took her to her mother. Just then a big boulder came crashing down right where the Chief had been standing. Then...a time traveler from the future went back to that very spot one day, before that occurrence, and stepped on and crushed that little butterfly..."

Tony cuts him off. "Okay, okay, I get it. The little girl had no butterfly to chase and didn't bump into the Chief, so he didn't move and the boulder hit and killed him. Right?"

Roger Dane walks over and finishes the story. "Exactly. And the resulting paradox created a domino effect that cascaded all the way to the twentieth century..."

Rye leans over and whispers into Tony's ear, ominously. "...And Adolf Hitler won World War Two."

Tony lets out a yelp. "Now that scares me! That really scares me!"

Audra rushes over and reprimands Rye and Roger.

"Now stop that, you two! Tony, don't worry about a thing. Just do whatever Frank tells you to do." She turns to the others. "Let's get ready for this test."

"Let's synchronize our chronometers." Frank commands. "Coming up to fifteen hundred hours... mark...now! Let's go!"

Tony jokes. "Hey! Mine says three o'clock in the afternoon."

They all turn and look at him. Tony just chuckles and shrugs.

The Observers follow Roger to the Control Area. Frank, Rye and Tony move to the central platform with their equipment. Audra follows Frank to give him last minute instructions.

As the time travelers don and check their equipment, the laboratory becomes a beehive of activity. Technicians activate the accelerators and start the spatial distortion. The silky gossamer-like spiraling wormhole appears in the central area in front of the Time Team.

Audra advises, "In approximately one half hour, we'll let our visitors go through the vortex for a quick look. So, during this test the wormhole will remain open the entire time you are all out there. Please be careful."

Frank and Audra look at each other knowingly. They'll need the extra power of these accelerators as well as the prehistoric electrical storm to generate and maintain a second vortex. That's one of the reasons why she's leaving the wormhole open. Actually, it's the main reason. Rye looks at both of them. He now understands how this will work.

As Audra returns to the Control Area, Frank fingers his special activator tucked in his pocket then straightens his gear and his extra equipment bag, or "Boy Scout Kit".

Roger activates the small negative accelerator overhead. Everyone looks up at the whirring sound. The time travelers secure their gear and get ready to move.

"The wormhole is stable. Time Travelers go!" Roger tells them.

Frank, Rye and Tony take a step into the silky vortex and disappear.

The three time travelers exit the wormhole and are standing on the prehistoric plateau five million years in the past. They all stand motionless, in awe of their surroundings. It's a clear day, but the dark storm clouds are moving rapidly in their direction.

Frank checks his chronometer and this time he knows they're in the right place and time period. He nods his head in approval and starts walking toward the edge of the plateau. Rye Michaels follow him, but a camera-laden Tony Joshua remains motionless.

Rye yells at him. "Tony! What's wrong? Y'all okay?"

"No!" Tony screams. "I'm scared shitless!"

"There's nothing to be afraid of." Frank tries to reassure him.

Tony points at a large animal that voraciously gobbles huge bugs and beetles. "Oh yeah! Look at that monster beast eating those humongous bugs. Am I next?"

"Not unless you're a bug. That's a giant sloth. They're not carnivorous." Frank says.

Tony still hesitates. "He might have a meat-eating cousin."

Frank gets irritated and snaps at him. "Go film from the top of that sun dial-shaped rock over there. Now!"

Tony mumbles as he moves cautiously toward the rock. "Nice little butterflies... Please stay away little butterflies."

The storm rapidly moves closer. Lightning flashes and thunder claps. A storm cloud moves in front of the sun and it grows darker. Rye stays close to Frank.

"You don't need to go with me." He tells Rye. "You can record from up here."

Rye disagrees. "No, I'm going with you." He wants to watch Frank's every move.

Frank stares at him for a long moment then relents. "Suit yourself." As he starts down into the valley that is partially blanketed with an eerie mist, Rye is right on his heels.

Frank knows that Rye is on a guilt trip because of Patty's death, and that if push comes to shove, Rye will back him up to save Patty. At least, he knows that's what Rye would have done in the past. He's not too certain now, but he may have to chance it.

Lightning flashes and thunder claps as the storm moves ever closer. They rub their arms and the back of their necks as the electricity in the air makes their hair stand on end.

Tony climbs onto the large rock at the edge of the plateau and sets out his camera equipment. Then he lays down on the rock and begins filming the valley below. He puts down one camera and picks up a video camcorder. He sees amazing varieties of animals, birds and vegetation as he films, and hears all the strange noises being made. Tony gets a little nervous and fumbles around with his equipment as he looks up at the sky and the oncoming storm.

Then he hears noises in the direction of the wormhole. Roger Dane and the Observers are standing in front of the wormhole in their blue jumpsuits. Tony aims his camcorder in their direction and films them. The Observers move away from the vortex very excited and overwhelmed at what they are seeing. Roger points to the oncoming storm as the lightning flashes. The loud thunder makes Roger turn and walk back to the vortex with the Observers close behind him. They all step into the wormhole and disappear.

In the valley below, Frank and Rye move slowly through the giant foliage, carefully watching their footing as they go. Frank starts to move faster toward some large trees. Rye notices this and tries to keep up with him. Frank cautions him:

"Don't move so fast. You might step on a butterfly."

Rye responds. "Well, y' all are moving faster." He knows Frank is trying to shake him.

"I know where I'm going. Go around the other side of those trees. I'll meet you there." Frank insists.

Rye hesitates momentarily then moves in that direction.

Frank quickly steps behind a big clump of trees, takes out the Special Activator from his pocket, looks back to make sure Rye can't see him then he activates the device.

A second wormhole appears.

Rye sees the area light up and tries to get a closer look.

Frank moves toward the new vortex, but suddenly a close lightning flash strikes nearby knocking the device from his hand.

The wormhole disappears. Rye is also a little stunned by the lightning strike but he still moves closer.

Frank picks up the device and sees that it's burned.

Rye yells at him. "Frank! I can't see you. Move out into the open."

Frank can't get the wormhole back, so he steps out from behind the trees and waves at Rye. Lightning flashes all over the area now and the storm moves rapidly over them. Frank then steps back behind the trees and tries to get the activator to work again without luck. He opens it then pulls out a blown fuse and holds it up. Frustrated, he pounds on the tree with his fist. Rye is wondering what happened and moves a little faster toward Frank.

Meanwhile up on the sundial rock, Tony jumps as bright lightning flashes directly overhead, followed immediately by very loud thunderclaps that jolt him. He drops a piece of his equipment, grabs for it, loses his balance and falls off the rock.

Frank and Rye are startled as they see Tony falling off the rock screaming and sliding down the slope. Tony grabs onto a large pointed rock and hangs on for dear life. As Frank and Rye start moving toward him, Tony's rock gives way and pulls out of the ground. Tony and the rock careen down the slope and come to rest right in front of them.

Thousands of giant roaches pour out of the hole left by the rock. The three time travelers stare at the giant cockroaches in horror.

Tony starts to frantically stomp on them. "Cockroaches! I hate cockroaches!"

Frank dives and tackles Tony and throws him to the ground. "Don't do that! Don't kill anything!"

"Hey! Those aren't <u>butterflies</u>! They're <u>cockroaches</u>!" Tony insists.

Frank moans and slaps his forehead.

Then the giant sloth comes down the hill and starts feasting on the cockroaches.

Frank looks shocked. "We'd better go back home and make sure things are okay." He moves up the hill with Rye and Tony following him. They occasionally look back and watch the giant sloth ravenously gobbling up the cockroaches.

They reach the top as it starts raining harder and the wind begins to blow more severely. They walk toward the wormhole when suddenly a series of severe lightning strikes flash all around them. Everyone dives for cover.

Rye takes out his chronometer and checks it against the wormhole, which is now flickering. "The wormhole is stable but losing power and seems to be deteriorating."

Frank does the same then says, "Something's wrong. It looks like this electrical storm is keeping it stable. We'd better go back and check everything right away."

Suddenly Tony realizes something. "Wait! I left my stuff on that rock."

 "Leave it!" Frank yells at him. "There's not enough time."

Tony starts running back to the sundial rock. Its raining harder and he slips and slides in the mud. Rye moves toward the wormhole. Frank starts after Tony.

"Tony, we don't have time! We have to go now! We'll get it later!" Frank yells.

Tony climbs up on the sundial rock and grabs his equipment. He looks back at the wormhole and sees Rye disappear into the vortex. Frank is now moving back toward the wormhole himself.

Tony screams, "Hey! Wait! Don't leave me here! Hey!"

He jumps down off the rock and runs frantically toward the wormhole. He is clinging to his equipment and running awkwardly, slipping and sliding in the mud.

Frank stops at the wormhole and waits a moment. Then he waves at Tony and steps into the vortex. In a panic and screaming, Tony dives headlong into the diminishing wormhole.

Rye is standing in the middle of an abandoned laboratory as Frank steps out of the wormhole onto the central platform. It's near dark, but a few boarded-up windows let in a little light. Everything is covered with dust and cobwebs. A clock ticks somewhere in this eerily quiet room. A dusty calendar on the wall reads, "May, 2000". Frank checks his chronometer and sees that it reads, "November, 2000". This lab was abandoned back in May he surmises.

"Where did everyone go?" asks Rye.

Frank is just as puzzled as he begins to examine everything.

Suddenly a mud-covered Tony comes flying out of the vortex sprawling onto the floor. The wormhole begins to diminish and flicker then it disappears. All is quiet.

"Hey! Why didn't you guys wait for me? I could've been killed. I could have been stranded. Jeez!" Tony yells at them.

Frank goes over and flips a circuit breaker turning on some lights. It looks a lot like the TX-7 Laboratory, but somewhat different. The large accelerators look almost the same. Frank goes over and examines the control panel. Tony picks himself up off the floor and starts cleaning the mud off himself and his equipment.

Rye moves to the central platform and replays his recordings. "I filmed the TX-7 Laboratory before we left to use as a comparison." He says. Rye views the replay in a small screen of his recorder as he compares it with this laboratory. He looks up but can't find the small accelerator, then sees it mounted off to the side. He looks up and sees a sign.

The sign reads "PROJECT SOUTH STAR" with graffiti over it marked "ABORTED".

Rye comments, "South Star? Our Project is TX-7. What's this?"

I guess we landed in someone else's laboratory." Tony says. "What does South Star mean?" He asks Frank.

A South Star is a Nova." Frank tells him.

Tony scratches his head. "Isn't that an exploding star?"

"No." Frank corrects, and then explains to him. "An exploding star is a Super Nova. A South Star or Nova is a star that suddenly increases greatly in brightness, then within a few years, or a few months, grows dim again. A South Star is also a person who only gets fifteen minutes of fame. Or like a Rock Group or a Singer with a single hit, or a One-Hit-Wonder. South Star is also used to describe the short-lived Confederacy of the 1860's."

Frank's last remark about the Confederacy makes Rye Michaels wince and scowl.

Tony thinks for a minute then he smiles and comments.

"Hey Hey! That's just like you two guys. Frank has an explosive Super Nova type personality, and Rye Michaels is a slow burner South Star Nova type from the South kinda like..."

Frank explodes again. "Never mind psychoanalyzing us! Just help us!"

"Okay, okay! I'm ready. Let's do it!" Tony moves away and walks over to turn on a TV set as Rye and Frank continue their examinations.

The TV set comes on with the evening news. The Newscaster is talking as Tony turns up the sound. "...And President Clinton, in his speech to the

Confederate party, told them how very proud he was to be a Confederate..."

Tony scratches his head, "Hey! I thought Clinton was a Democrat."

Frank quickly runs over and turns off the TV set. "Never mind! Just keep cleaning up."

Rye begins double-checking his recordings concerning the small accelerator, while Frank pulls out and closely examines their Operations Manual. Tony walks to a desk, picks up and dusts off a History book like the one that Audra always shows everyone. The cover title reads, "History Of The United States Of America". Tony skims through it then looks confused. He waves the history book at them and says:

"Man! This history book is really screwed up. This says there are three political parties: Democrat, Republican and... Confederate Party!"

Rye grabs the book from him and starts looking through it. He looks surprised at first, then alarmed. He slams the book down on the desk and grabs Tony by the collar.

"You idiot, Joshua! You killed those prehistoric cockroaches and changed history! We warned you about that!" Rye screams.

Tony panics, grabs the history book and frantically flips through the pages. He gets to the page titled "World War II" and sees the headlines "Allies Win". He lets out a sigh of relief.

Frank is looking upward searching for the small accelerator. "Don't worry about it, Rye! We can correct the problem by going back to prehistory earlier and preventing Tony from falling off that sundial rock." He tells them.

When Tony hears Frank's solution to the problem he relaxes. Frank is still looking upward. "Where in the hell is that small negative Accelerator?"

Rye taps him on the shoulder and points down front. Frank nods and heads for it.

"I wonder how many Time Travelers they lost with this small negative accelerator mounted in the wrong place." Frank tells them. Tony responds as he looks at some photos on the wall. "According to this, they lost three."

Rye and Frank walk over and look over Tony's shoulder. Three photos are crossed out with dates written under each. The graffiti over them reads, "Lost In Time". None of the lost time travelers look anything like Frank, Rye or Tony.

"I don't recognize any of them or their names." Frank says.

Then all three turn and look back at the small accelerator.

"Let's Move it!"

Frank unhooks it. Tony gets a ladder. Rye helps Frank carry the accelerator underneath some overhead brackets then Frank carries it up the ladder and begins mounting it on the brackets.

Outside, two Security Guards walk to the front of the building and check the locked doors. They continue walking around the building, checking the rest of the boarded-up doors and windows.

One of the guards spots the lights shining through the boarded-up windows of the laboratory. He points to it and they go for a closer look. One takes out a cell phone and makes a call. The guards split up and go in different directions checking all the locked doors.

Soon, a hovercraft with a "Security" sign painted on the side flies up and lands. Several security guards exit the craft and quickly move toward the building entrance.

Frank finishes installing the small accelerator overhead and jumps down. Rye checks the position with his recorder. They nod to each other and head for the control panel. Frank turns on the power and types rapidly on the keyboard then activates the large accelerators. These accelerators start faster than their own. They seem to run much smoother and are up to full power in a shorter period of time.

Then the misty silky wormhole materializes so much faster than before, that it startles them. Frank quickly activates the small negative accelerator now mounted overhead and the wormhole stabilizes quickly. He nods and they all move toward the central platform.

"Check your chronometers now," Frank tells them, "And then again when we arrive on the prehistoric plateau to make sure we're in the right time period..."

Suddenly the power goes off and the accelerators begin to wind down. The wormhole disappears before they get to it. More lights come on and brighten up the entire area. Security guards charge into the lab followed by Roger Dane and Audra Ashley.

"Who are you people?" Roger asks. "What are you doing here?"

Roger and Audra are much healthier-looking and much better groomed now. They are also more stylishly dressed. Even the guards' uniforms are somewhat of a fashion statement.

Rye nudges Frank and points to the unusually slim and trim weapons held by the guards. Tony thinks fast and blurts out boisterously. "Your three missing time travelers have returned.

We look a little bit different now, but with some tender loving care, we should be just fine." Audra and Roger look at each other and then Audra turns to the guards.

"Arrest these imposters!"

The South Star detention cell is minimum security and Tony looks out the window while Frank paces back and forth in the cell. Rye is sitting on the bed reading the history book that Tony found on the desk in the laboratory.

"Listen to this." Rye tells them. "Their Civil War ended in a draw in 1863 with a Peace Agreement. That's two years before our Civil War ended."

"I don't want to hear about it!" Frank snaps at him.

"I do." Tony says. "This is all fascinating to me."

Rye ignores Frank and continues reading out loud to Tony. "Listen to this, Tony. The USA and the CSA continued on, side-by-side, as two Independent Nations for over seventy years, peacefully and competitively."

"Wow!" exclaims Tony. "The Confederate States Of America survived?"

Frank turns to them. "Not so good for the slaves."

"On the contrary!" Rye says quickly flipping through the pages. "Slavery was abolished in their Constitution of 1776, as part of their Declaration of Independence. There was no slavery here in their America!"

"No Slavery!! Wow! Wow! !" Tony exclaims wide-eyed.

Frank gets nervous and begins pacing again. Tony looks out the window. "You should see what it looks like outside now." He tells them. The buildings are more glamorously designed and a lot more colorfully decorated than the former steel and glass structures that were there when they left. The plaza area is beautifully and elaborately landscaped. Even though this complex has been abandoned, the plaza area and the grounds still look very well tended, and the buildings well maintained.

Rye continues reading out loud, "...and because of the Great Depression and the threat of World War Two, they re-united under Franklin Delano Roosevelt, and forming one united nation with a Three Party System..."

Frank spins round and yells at him. "Shut up! Just shut-the-fuck-up!!"

Tony walks over to read the book over Rye's shoulder. They lower their voices.

"So that's where the Confederate Party came from." Tony comments.

Rye enthusiastically flips through the pages. "All the U. S. Presidents were the same. Only their Party affiliations were different."

Tony gets more excited now. "Who were the Presidents of the Confederate States Of America, after the Civil War?" he wants to know.

Rye flips through the pages again and reads. "Let's see...uh...Jefferson Davis, Robert E. Lee, J.E.B. Stuart... Whoa! Jeb Stuart was killed near the end of our Civil War when..."

Frank rushes over and grabs the book from Rye's hands. "Will you two stop! We've got to get out of here and get back home."

Rye jumps up and angrily grabs the book back. "It looked to me like we <u>were</u> home! We all saw Roger Adam Dane and Audra Heather Ashley."

"They didn't recognize us. They are not the same people as before." Frank barks back. Tony begins to swagger around the cell in a cocky manner. "I changed history." He says. "I created a better world! Hey, baby will you look at me now-wow-wow..." Tony chirps.

Frank grabs the book from Rye and throws it at Tony. It misses him and slams against the wall. Tony jumps back and Rye laughs. Frank raises his hands in frustration.

In the South Star Laboratory, Roger and Audra anxiously examine the equipment belonging to the time travelers.

"This equipment is almost the same as ours." Audra comments. "Yet, it's not the same, somewhat different, minor variances...amazing."

Roger examines Frank's operations manual. "Audra! This manual has our names in it!" he exclaims disbelievingly. Audra quickly looks at it with Roger.

"This says Project TX-7." She says. "That means 'Time Travel Expedition Number Seven'. Their first six attempts failed."

"We know quite a bit about failed attempts." Roger remarks.

They look at each other then Audra starts for the door with Roger right on her heels.

"We must talk to these men now!" She exclaims.

In their cell, Rye continues reading the history book quietly to himself while Frank continues pacing back and forth. Tony looks out the window and marvels again at all the wondrous changes. "Everything looks cleaner and fresher, and all these people look a lot healthier than us." Tony says.

Frank stops pacing momentarily and ponders. "I noticed how different Audra looked."

Rye looks up from the book as Frank begins to pace again. "I've never seen Roger Adam Dane dressed so

stylishly." Rye comments.

"Hey! I worked on a movie set where all the actors looked glamorously picture-perfect." Tony tells them. "That's how all these people look to me now. `Hollywood Picture-Perfect'."

Rye holds up the history book with open pages showing photographs of very modern scenes. "According to these pictures and these descriptions, society is actually about thirty to fifty years better developed and more advanced than when we left." He stands up then walks to the window and looks out. "It must have been the competition between the USA and the CSA that made everything so much better." Rye suggests.

Frank stops pacing when he hears footsteps coming their way. Rye and Tony move away from the window as Roger and Audra, accompanied by several security guards, approach their cell. Roger carries Rye's recorder and Frank's manual. Audra has Frank's special activator.

"Gentlemen!" Audra addresses them. "We have some questions to ask you."

Tony comes running over and asks Audra a quick question through the bars. "We didn't kill off Santa Claus, did we? The kids would never forgive us if we did that! Jeez!" He says, gripping the bars of the cell door.

Rye starts laughing uproariously. Roger and Audra look at each other, puzzled.

"Tony, quit joking around!" Frank tells him.

"I'm not joking. I'm serious...Well did we?!! Tony insists.

Finally Audra understands what Tony is asking. "No, young man. Santa is still with us."

Tony breathes a big sigh of relief. Rye laughs even harder. Frank smiles a little.

Frank checks his wristwatch, being pressed for time, and gets nervous again. He moves closer to the door and tries to reach for his activator through the bars. Audra quickly draws back.

"I was just going to show you how that worked." Frank tells her.

"I'm sure you were. But, it doesn't work, since it has a blown fuse...and you knew that, didn't you?" She informs him.

Dismayed, Frank tries a different tack. "Excuse me, Audra...er...Doctor Ashley. Do you have a sister named Arriana?"

Audra looks surprised, but she responds. "Why, yes. She's married to a Senator...A Confederate Senator."

Both Frank and Rye reel back at this news. Frank is shaken, but Rye moves closer.

"Does she have a daughter named...Patricia?" Rye asks her.

Audra responds, "No. She has a son named Jeb."

Rye bursts out laughing. Frank turns and hits him, but Rye keeps laughing as he falls back onto the bed. Then he lashes out at Frank without thinking. "Y'all won't need that special activator now, Frank. Patty doesn't even exist in this place, so..."

Frank grabs him by the throat. "How do you know about that!" he demands.

Rye fights him off. "Back off! I know you want to go back and save Patty. I heard all about Audra's new gadget."

Audra looks stunned by Rye's remarks and she examines the activator more closely, wondering why he referred to her. Rye grabs the bars of the door and lashes out at them. "If you people want to find your lost time travelers, you'd better listen to us...By the way, did y'all have an engineer named Franklin Delano Zachary with your project?"

Audra and Roger take a good close look at Frank.

"No. Not that we know of." They respond.

"Well, that explains it." Rye muses.

Roger starts replaying Rye's recorder. He holds it up so they can see the small screen and the images rushing by. It shows the TX-7 Laboratory and the position of the small overhead accelerator. Then Roger comments, "I'm beginning to understand what's going on in your recordings, mister Michaels."

Rye snaps back, "You'll never understand. Your program failed. Our program succeeded. If y' all want our help..."

Frank grabs Rye to shut him up. "Don't say any more!"

Audra holds up a photograph of the small accelerator. "Is this the correct position for the Small Negative Accelerator?" she asks.

Silence.

Roger holds up some more photographs. "What is this unusual prehistoric-looking scenery in the background of these pictures?" he asks.
More silence.

"Gentlemen, if you want our help, you help us." she tells them.

She turns and leaves with Roger and the guards right behind her.

When they're gone, Frank admonishes Rye and Tony.

"Both of you keep your mouths shut! Don't give out any information. Do you hear me?"

"They said they'd help us if we helped them." Tony says.

Frank puts his hands on his hips. "Now that they've got this thing figured out, they're not going to let us go back."

"We may need to give them some information in order to cut some kind of deal." Rye tells him.

"No <u>Deals</u>!" Frank means every word.

Audra and Roger move the time travelers' equipment to a conference room and display it on a large table. Audra studies some more photos.

"I'm certain now that the position of that small negative accelerator makes all the difference." She says.

"We can't let those men go back and correct their problem." Roger tells her. "It may create problems for us."

Audra stringently objects. "Oh, but we must! They'll never agree to help us retrieve our lost men if we don't help them."

"Don't you see, Audra!" he says. "If they change history back to their way... <u>We may cease to Exist!</u>"

Later that night, Frank and Rye crouch on either side of their cell door while Tony starts rolling on the floor, a stack of empty dinner trays next to their beds. "Help me!" Tony moans. "I'm sick. What was in that food you gave us?"

The guards rush in to help Tony. Rye and Frank jump them and knock them out.

Tony gets up off the floor and the three of them quickly exit the cell after they tie and gag the guards. They move cautiously down the hall.

"One of the guards said they're keeping our gear in the Conference Room." Frank says. "We'll go there first and then to the Laboratory."

"I want to see more of what's outside." Rye tells him.

Frank warns, "Believe me, you're better off not knowing. Now, let's go get our `Boy Scout Kits'."

"Well, this explains why you packed all that extra gear." Rye says.

Frank quickly agrees believing that Rye doesn't suspect anything more. "Right!"

But Rye still has his own agenda. "You two have fun. I want a better look around outside. I'm heading for that exit." he tells them as he moves quickly toward the door.

"Hey! Wait for me!" Tony starts to follow Rye, but Frank grabs his arm.

"If you go out there, you may not make it back home." Frank warns him. Tony thinks about that for a moment then decides to stay with Frank.

Rye stops at the exit and waves back at them.

"Adios!"

Rye leaves the building and moves cautiously through the bushes toward an alley. He dives for cover when a guard on patrol comes around the corner. After the guard passes by, Rye runs to the alley and disappears into the night.

Frank moves down the hallway with Tony right behind him. They stop at a supply room. Frank opens the door and examines the equipment consisting of mops, buckets, brooms and other cleaning equipment. Suddenly they hear footsteps as a couple of guards come their way. Frank and Tony quickly jump into the supply room and close the door behind them.

Frank examines some coveralls that are hanging on a hook. They are dark brown and fit right over their own khaki coveralls. He and Tony put them on. They both pick up mops and buckets then open the door and peek out. The hallway looks clear so they venture out cautiously.

Then Tony accidentally steps on the mop and trips, dropping the bucket with a big bang. They grab everything and jump back into the supply room, quickly closing the door. They peek out again. No one is around. They venture out again, very carefully this time.

Rye runs down to the end of the alleyway, ducking in and out of trashcans and dumpsters, trying to keep out of the lighted up areas. A police car turns down the alley and Rye dives into one of the dumpsters. After the patrol car is gone, he climbs out and continues down the alley.

Frank and Tony make their way down the hall. A guard escorts a group of well-dressed people down the hall in their direction. Frank and Tony mop the floor until the group passes by.

"We sure started things going around here again." he tells Tony.

The guard escorts the people into the Conference Room. Frank can see into the room through the hallway window. He sees Audra so they head in that direction. Then every time someone comes by, he and Tony stop and mop the floor again.

Audra leads everyone out of the Conference Room and into the Laboratory. Frank and Tony wait until it's clear then they quickly head for the Conference Room. They sneak in and check their gear. Frank goes directly to his Boy Scout Kit and makes certain everything he needs is still there. He finds everything he needs and they start to leave, but a security guard enters looking for something and they have to duck under the conference table. The guard picks up an item of equipment and quickly exits without noticing them. Frank and Tony wait a moment then they exit carefully and return to the supply room. They close the door behind them leaving it open slightly so they can see down the hallway. Whenever someone walks by, they close the door and wait until whoever it is has passed by.

After a while, Audra and the guests exit the Laboratory and walk down the hall. The guards turn out the lights then close the doors and leave. When it's clear, Frank and Tony come out of the supply room and sneak into the Laboratory. The night-light is on in the empty room.

Frank moves fast to the control panel, turns on the computer and types on the keyboard.

He calls up his previous settings and the program appears on the computer screen. He motions to Tony to go to the Central Platform and Tony complies.

Frank opens his gear bag and takes out several items. He puts the lock-picks in a pocket in his sleeve. He puts several items in other pockets then he opens a large drawer of the console and hides the rest of the gear inside. Then he returns to his program. He activates the large accelerators. They begin to hum and he turns the power up full. When the vortex appears he activates the small negative accelerator overhead. When the wormhole stabilizes, Frank motions to Tony and they swiftly move toward the vortex.

All at once Roger Dane and several Security Guards enter quickly from another room through a different side-door and intercept them.

"I'm terribly sorry, Gentlemen, but we can't allow you to leave just yet." Roger says.

Frank and Tony freeze when the guards come at them. That's when Frank notices the newly mounted security cameras over the doors. He tries to make excuses. "I'm very sorry to disappoint you, Doctor Dane, but we were merely going to test the space-time differential."

Security Guards on either side of them grab them both by the arms. Frank and Tony suddenly use their karate and drop all the guards quickly. Other guards draw weapons and surround them. Frank raises his hands over his head and gives up. Tony follows suit. Roger tries to reassure them, "Believe me, we mean you no harm."

Frank lashes out in desperation and tries to grab Dane before the guards stop him.

"Then let me go back! My daughter's life is at stake!" Frank bellows out angrily.

Rye Michaels wakes up in a dumpster seeing daylight. He's covered from head to foot with grease and grime that was in the dumpster's trash where he slept. He rants and raves and cusses as he climbs out and tries to clean himself off. Then he turns and kicks the dumpster. He makes his way down the alley toward a cross street. When he reaches the street, he carefully looks up and down before he continues onward cautiously.

As he comes around the corner, he stops and gawks at the appearance of these buildings and shops, they have a greater colorful and futuristic construction and design than his own. Even this seeming 'skid-row' area is much cleaner and brighter looking than some of his-own nicer neighborhoods. He stops for a time and marvels at these new surroundings.

Rye spots a Pawn Shop and heads for it as he removes his wristwatch. Two policemen on foot patrol come around the corner and Rye instinctively jumps into an alley until they pass then he continues on. He looks around surreptitiously then quickly enters `El Rey's Pawn Shop'.

Frank and Tony are back in the detention cell at the South Star facility. Frank paces back and forth as Tony once again looks out the window.

Audra pays them a visit. She holds up Frank's special activator, which has now been well repaired, making it look almost brand new. "I'm sorry to hear about your daughter, Mr. Zachary." she says to him with sympathy. "I assume that's what this special activator was for. You were trying to go back to save her."

Frank nods and tries to reach for it again. She moves back. Frank lowers his head. "I'll make you a deal, Doctor Ashley. I'll help you find your missing time travelers if you help us get back home."

Tony spins around. "Hey! I thought you said no deals!"

"That was before Rye Michaels ran off. Things have changed now." Frank tells him.

Audra moves closer. "I'm listening. Tell me more."

Rye Michaels argues with the pawnbroker in the pawnshop. In a rage, Rye accepts the money and storms out of 'El Rey's Pawn Shop'. He stops outside, picks up a rock and thinks about throwing it through the pawnshop window.

But then he notices something unusual about the money he's holding in his hand. He studies the money and holds up one of the bills. It's a One Hundred Dollar bill, but on this one there's a picture of Robert E. Lee. Rye smiles and drops the rock. He puts the money in his pocket and continues on his way. Then he looks up at a flagpole on the front of one of the buildings. On it is a flag with a very unusual and colorful combination of the Stars and Stripes (USA) and the Stars and Bars (CSA). It's a very beautiful, venerable and dignified flag of the United States of America denoting Unity.

Rye smiles broadly and continues down the street.

Frank stands at the controls in the South Star laboratory with Audra at his side. Tony is sitting at a nearby table. Roger Dane enters carrying three dossiers and hands them to Frank. He examines them, selects one and gives it to Audra. She nods in agreement and they move to the computers. Frank hands her a sheet of paper with figures on it.

Audra types on the computer while referring to the sheet of paper. She enters figures while Roger looks over her shoulder and then they study the results. Frank then moves to another keyboard and begins typing rapidly. They watch every move he makes closely, but he types in code. As soon as they look away, he puts in some new figures then quickly codes them.

Audra believes they're ready. "Let's give it a try. Everyone get ready!"

Roger activates the accelerators. Audra stands at the control panel and types, while Frank stands at the other one. Two technicians carry a portable mobile communicator to the central platform. The wormhole materializes. Roger then activates the small negative accelerator, which is now properly mounted overhead and the wormhole stabilizes. Audra quickly types some figures then nods. Frank types in another set of figures and nods. The technicians push the mobile locator-communicator into the wormhole and it disappears.

"Okay, dial the number." Roger tells them. Audra types on the computer. They all look at the clock on the wall. All watch the wormhole and the second hand of the clock as it ticks off the seconds. Suddenly they pick up a return signal. Excitedly they send a message back. They wait. Soon, another signal returns.

Everyone starts cheering and dancing around.

"We've made contact with Jones and he has the coordinates!" Audra excitedly exclaims. "Now he can

locate the wormhole." She says as she covers her tears with her hands.

In all the excitement, no one notices as Frank reaches into the console where he stashed his gear and begins pocketing certain items, including one of the South Star standard activators.

Roger shuts down the accelerators and the vortex disappears.

"We'll re-activate first thing in the morning. That will give Jones time to reach the communicator." Roger tells everyone.

Audra adds, "I'm certain that he'll find it now. We shall retrieve him tomorrow. Have a good day everyone!"

As the guards escort Frank and Tony out, Frank sees Audra lock his special activator in the drawer of her console. He takes note of this and fingers the lock-pick in his sleeve.

Rye walks down the busy downtown street and marvels at the people and their styles. He stops at a Men's Clothing Store and studies the fashions in the window. People walk by and stare at him in his greasy coveralls. He sticks out his tongue and throws them the finger, then he enters `Joel and Andrews Men's Wear' clothing store.

The owners greet him. "Hi! We are Joel and Andrew. May we help you?" "Yes, y'all certainly may!" Rye smiles and flashes his cash.

Frank and Tony enter their detention cell and sit down on their beds. The guards lock the cell door securely and leave. Frank gets up and paces back and forth while Tony goes to the window again.

"We've got to do something about those security cameras in the Laboratory."

Tony offers, "Let's cover them with a bag."

"No. When the screens go dark, the guards will come running. We need to record a program showing the Laboratory empty with the nightlights on, then keep it running in a continuous loop on their monitors." Frank tells him.

"How do we do that?"

"We'll go to their Security Office and rig some discs." Frank says.

"Gee! That sounds easy. Let's just trot on down there right now." Tony jokes.

"Very funny. Get some rest. You'll need it tonight." Frank lies down on his bunk.

"I don't need any rest." Tony tells him.

"Just go to bed so the guards will leave us alone." Frank insists.

Tony stares out the window for a while longer then he goes to bed.

Rye Michaels, now clean and more fashionably dressed, goes into the Public Library and heads for the Confederate History section. He picks out several books, some CD's and DVD's and sits at a table with a TV set. He opens a large history book on the Confederacy and when he looks up, he sees a very stunningly beautiful blonde lady walking his way, with a very bright smile on her face.

"How do you do, Sir. I'm Annabelle Lee Stephens. I see that you are interested in Confederate History. I helped categorize this entire section, of which we are very proud, and I shall be very happy to assist you in any way." She chirps with a melodious Confederate accent.

Rye is stunned to hear the name Annabelle Lee Stephens, which was the name of the girl who was, murdered with Lucy Belle Michaels shortly after the Civil War...the cause of the black cloud over the Michaels Family. Also, this lady's beauty seemed to render him speechless.

Annabelle continues, "Actually, I'm at the main library in Atlanta, Georgia, but I'm here in Denver temporarily to assist this department with some new entries. I certainly hope I can assist you with whatever you may like to know."

Rye stammers, "Ah...You said your name was Annabelle Lee... Stephens? He asks.

"Why, yes. Actually, I am a direct descendent of Alexander Hamilton Stephens, the first Vice-President of the Confederate States Of America." She informs him. How do you do Miss Stephens...I...I just wanted to catch up..." Rye tells her.

"Certainly." She says, as she inserts one of the discs into the TV.

Rye sits back to watch and listen, often glancing sideways at the beautiful Annabelle.

On the TV, the narrator says: "...And after Robert E. Lee died in office, his Vice-President, the very dashing and flamboyant James Ewell Brown (JEB) Stuart, became the third and youngest President of the Confederate States of America, ushering in a fabulous period of prosperity never before seen..."

Rye stands up and apologizes, "I'm sorry, Miss Stephens, but I'm late for a meeting. Will you please excuse me? I must go now, but I shall return. If I miss you here, perhaps I'll see you in Atlanta."

Annabelle smiles, "Why, how charming, sir. However... You have the strangest accent."

"Oh...ah...We call it a Southern Accent." Rye explains.

"My word, from how far south do you hail, with such a harsh and gruff accent?" she asks.

"Ah...about as far as South America?" Rye remembers that his great-granddaddy had a twin brother who traveled to South America and was never heard from again.

"Fascinating!" she remarks. "I am certain that we shall meet again."

"I certainly hope so." Rye says.

Rye turns and walks toward the door with his brow furrowed.

"I've got to stop Frank from Destroying all this!" he says to himself.

He rushes out of the library.

Audra and Roger are closing down the laboratory and getting ready to leave.

"I now know what Franklin Zachary has done." Audra says. "This end of the wormhole is stable because of the large accelerators here in the Laboratory. However, the other end of the vortex is unstable so the tail wobbles and may jump from one location to another, or even from one time period to another. By correctly adjusting the smaller negative accelerator overhead, it stabilizes the whole wormhole.

Roger comments, "Yes, I see. But, he has deleted his programs each time."

Audra unlocks the drawer of her console, takes out Frank's special activator and puts it in her pocket then re-locks the drawer. "I don't believe he has deleted his programs. Those calculations would be too difficult to re-program each time." She says. "I believe they're still in our computer somewhere. We simply need his codes."

"I'll put our best computer experts on it right away." Roger says.

Then Audra reflects a bit. "Before they time traveled, Frank was married to my sister Arriana and they had a daughter named Patricia." She pauses, then "I think it's about time I gave my sister Arri a call."

Rye Michaels hides behind a tree in the front plaza of the South Star facility. He pulls out a pistol and attaches a silencer to the barrel.

A Security hovercraft glides up and lands. Several security guards exit the craft and walk toward the main entrance.

Rye moves back into the shadows until they've all entered the building then he moves quickly toward a side door.

Audra and Roger exit the Laboratory and head down the hall. After they pass by the detention cell, Frank comes to the door and watches them leave. He moves back when a guard walks by and looks in on them then moves on. After the guard leaves, Frank goes back to the door, looks up and down the hallway to make certain it's clear then goes over and shakes Tony.

"Come on. Let's go!"

Tony rubs the sleep from his eyes. "So, soon? I just got to sleep."

"Hurry up. We don't have much time."

Frank lifts the mattress and pulls out several blankets and another pair of dark brown maintenance coveralls. Tony does the same. They take off their khaki coveralls, stuff them with blankets and arrange them in their beds to look like they're still sleeping. Frank transfers his gear to the dark brown maintenance coveralls and puts them on, as does Tony. Then Frank pulls out the lock pick, unlocks the cell door and they move out into the hall. He re-locks the door and they continue toward the Security office. They can see the screens monitoring the Laboratory through the hall window. The guards leave the Security Office to greet the new guards coming in from the hovercraft and take them to the Laboratory.

Frank and Tony sneak into the monitoring room and search through the recording discs. They find the ones they want and insert them into the Lab's security monitors. They start the programs and set them to re-play so that the Lab looks empty all the time then they leave just before the guards return.

After the guards leave the Laboratory, Frank and Tony enter and lock the doors behind them. "Let's lock and block all the doors this time." Frank says. Tony moves to take care of the other side doors while Frank goes to the control panel and starts typing to call up his special programs. He checks his figures with his chronometer and a hand calculator then adjusts one of their standard activators. He hooks them on a utility belt along with a flashlight and weapons then straps it around his waist. Tony follows suit.

Frank picks the lock on Audra's console, but he can't find his special activator. He pounds his fist on the desk and slams the drawer shut leaving it <u>unlocked.</u> He zips up his coveralls and goes to the central platform. He clicks the standard activator and the large accelerators activate and hum as they come to full power. He clicks it again and the small accelerator turns on and whirs. The wormhole appears and stabilizes quickly.

He motions to Tony and they both step into the wormhole and disappear.

On the prehistoric plateau, five million years in the past, Frank and Tony step out of the wormhole into the moonlight.

"Oh, great!" Frank exclaims. "It's three o'clock in the <u>morning</u> instead of afternoon."

"What do we do now?" Tony asks. "Wait here for another twelve hours?"

"No, we can't stay away from the Laboratory that long. The security programs will shut off automatically in one hour." He tells Tony.

Frank switches on the flashlight and checks his chronometer then he walks to the spot of the first wormhole. Tony switches on his flashlight and follows him. "Twelve hours from now, you, me and Rye Michaels should come out of the TX-7 wormhole right here." Frank tells him. Then he walks to the edge of the plateau with Tony right behind him.

Frank shines his light down into the valley. They see the pointed rock that Tony overturned and it is still intact. Then they hear the roar of a night predatory animal coming toward them and they both freeze.

Tony begins shaking, "Whatever that is, it sounds hungry and we're dinner."

"That's another reason we don't have much time. Let's hurry!" Frank says.

Frank moves to the sundial rock that Tony fell off of and examines it closely. He looks around and motions toward a large fallen tree branch. "Help me drag that tree branch over to the sundial rock." Frank tells him.

Tony immediately understands. "Hey, yeah! If I have something to grab onto, I won't fall off that rock and kill those cockroaches."

They hear another roar getting closer and both move faster. They carry the tree branch to the sundial rock and prop it up to where Tony will be standing. They then tie it down with a piece of vine and make sure it's secure. Another roar is very close now and Tony takes off running for the wormhole. Frank finishes strapping the branch and runs for the vortex, as well.

Tony jumps into the wormhole. Frank runs to the wormhole as the beast closes in on him then quickly jumps into it and disappears.

Frank exits the wormhole into the South Star Laboratory and clicks the activator causing the wormhole to disappear and the accelerators to shut down. Tony is sitting on the floor catching his breath. Frank goes to the control panel and closes down all the programs. They unblock and unlock all the doors and get ready to leave.

Rye Michaels arrives at the detention cell inside the South Star facility and peeks in the door. He sees what he thinks are Frank and Tony asleep in their beds. He's not sure which is which, so he pulls out the pistol with the silencer and through the bars of the cell door he fires three shots into each bed. Then he quickly moves back down the hall toward the exit.

Frank and Tony go to the Laboratory door. Frank checks the security camera and the clock on the wall to make sure they still have time. Tony checks the hallway then he jumps back in as someone is coming his way...that someone being Rye Michaels on his way out... but Tony doesn't recognize him. They wait until they hear Rye pass by then they open the door and cautiously enter the hall. Both Frank and Tony hurry toward the Security Office to deactivate the monitor programs, but there are too many guards in there now.

"Now What?" Tony asks.

Frank reassures him, "The program should automatically shut off in half an hour. Let's just go back to our detention cell." They by-pass Security and go directly to their cell.

Tony heads for his bed as Frank starts to re-lock the door. Tony throws back his blanket and lets out a scream. "Hey! Somebody put holes in my blanket!"

Frank immediately checks the beds. "Those are bullet holes. Put everything back the way it was and let's get out of here."

Tony panics and runs for the door. "Someone's trying to kill us. I'm out of here!"

He charges out the door and down the hall at a run. Frank chases after him leaving the cell door unlocked. As Tony reaches the exit door, Frank yells to him. "Wait

Let's go back to the Laboratory and get out of here that way." But Tony is already out the door and gone.

Frank goes back to the Laboratory.

Tony flies out the door and frantically runs to the alley in a panic, never looking back. Two guards come around the corner of the building, but Tony is already down the alley before they even notice. He runs down the alley terrified, occasionally looking back over his shoulder. He stays out of the lighted areas and just keeps moving.

Frank enters the Laboratory and locks the door. He checks the security camera and the wall clock to make sure he has enough time. He goes to the console drawer where he stashed his gear and takes out his 'Boy Scout kit'. He spreads everything out and picks out the equipment he needs. He grabs a ladder and moves it under the small negative accelerator then climbs the ladder and takes out an explosive device along with a remote control detonator.

Frank attaches the explosives on top of the small negative accelerator out of sight. He takes out the detonator to test it, but it slips from his hand and drops to the floor. Frank cringes. He climbs down, picks up the detonator and checks it over. He climbs the ladder again and successfully tests it this time, telling himself he must slow down.

Tony comes to a cross street and looks around the building. He sees a pawnshop still open and cautiously moves in that direction taking off his wristwatch. After looking around to make certain he's not being followed, he enters 'Meredith's Pawn Shop'.

Frank climbs onto a table where he can see the bomb on top of the small accelerator. He flips the switch on the detonator that activates red lights on both the detonator and the explosive device. All he has to do now is press the button. He flips the switch off and both lights go out. He puts the detonator in his pocket, climbs down off the table and puts the ladder back then he goes to the control panel.

Tony comes out of 'Meredith's Pawn Shop' counting his money. Then he looks up and is very surprised to see the "NOVA LOUNGE" across the street. He runs across without looking and almost gets hit by a car. He straightens himself out and enters the Nova Lounge.

The decor is different but the atmosphere is almost the same as their own Nova Lounge. The bartender is older and smokes a cigar. The clock on the wall with the swinging pendulum lights up the face like a star going Nova as before.

Tony is amazed when he sees the same old drunk sitting on the same bar stool staring straight ahead in that identical catatonic state. Tony sits next to him.

"Some people never change." Tony muses.

The bartender chomps down on his cigar and checks out the coveralls Tony is wearing.

"We don't serve no bums here." He says.

Tony puts his money on the bar. The bartender nods and Tony orders a drink.

Frank is at the control panel in the Laboratory and starts to re-activate his programs, but a security alarm goes off down the hall.

"They've found our bullet-riddled beds." He makes certain everything is shut off then runs to a ventilator shaft, climbs up on the table, opens the screen and crawls in closing the screen behind him.

Now he waits and watches.

Meanwhile at the Nova Lounge, the bartender quickly hangs up the telephone as Tony comes staggering out of the Men's Room. Tony plops down beside the old drunk.

The old drunk, speaking in that same monotone voice, says to him, "So, you traveled back in time, stepped on a cockroach and when you returned, everything was different. Right?"

Tony takes a deep breath and lets out a big sigh. "Well, that blonde at the end of the bar is just as beautiful as ever, but you and the bartender are a lot uglier now."

The bartender laughs nervously. Tony glances back at the Men's Room, "Now, where was I before I had to go take a pee?"

The old drunk responds, "Let's see...you and your brother Sam have different fathers, but the same mother. She's a character actress in Hollywood and you're both black belts in karate..."

That last statement makes the bartender nervous. The old drunk continues, "You've decided to dress up in women's clothing, like you did with the paparazzi, whatever that is, and fly back to Hollywood to make Lauriena Sue Moreaux world famous again, like you did before..."

Tony takes another deep breath. "Jeez! How long have I been here?"

"About two and a half hours." the bartender answers.

"And I said all that?"

"Yep.

Suddenly the doors burst open and the South Star security guards charge in and grab Tony. The bartender ducks down behind the bar. The old drunk just keeps staring straight ahead. Tony uses his karate and knocks down two or three of the guards, but he's too drunk to fight back effectively and they soon subdue him.

As they haul Tony out, one of the guards pays off the bartender.

A very upset and sad looking Audra Ashley enters the South Star Laboratory and goes to her console. She takes out Frank's special activator from her pocket and sets it on top then takes out her keys to open the drawer. To her surprise she finds the drawer open. She looks around suspiciously.

Roger Dane enters looking very troubled. "I don't know what we'll do now. I guess we'll have to forget about Jones and the others..."

"Oh, Roger, be quiet!" Audra admonishes. "Let's just do it ourselves."

He shrugs and goes to the control panel. "All right, everyone. Take your places!"

From behind the screen of the ventilation shaft, Frank watches their every move as the whole laboratory comes alive. Roger activates the accelerators. The wormhole appears and stabilizes. Audra types rapidly on her keyboard. They wait.

Suddenly a man steps out of the wormhole carrying the locator-communicator. Audra recognizes their missing time traveler and yells out.

"Eureka! It's Jones!" She throws her arms around him and gives him a big hug. Everyone cheers.

Frank re-positions himself so that he can see all that's happening in the Laboratory. He takes the remote detonator from his pocket and flips the switch. The red light on the detonator goes on and from here he can see the red light on top of the small accelerator light up. He flips off the switch and both red lights go out. He puts the detonator back in his pocket.

Audra is at her computer typing on the keyboard when her sister, Arriana, enters. Arriana is very chic, fashionably dressed and more glamorous than before.

"Audra, tell me more about this secret mission you want me to do. It sounds terribly exciting." Arri gushes out.

"Oh dear, not now, Arriana. Please." Audra says looking up from her work.

Looking through the screen of the ventilation shaft, Frank is flabbergasted when he sees Arriana enter. He leans forward and pushes his face against the screen for a closer look. He pushes harder against the screen trying to see her better. Abruptly the screen pops open and Frank goes flying out headfirst. He bounces off the table where he climbed up and then lands sprawling on the floor with a big thud, startling everyone. He takes the detonator out of his pocket and hides it under a nearby console. Then he stands up brushing himself off as the security guards close in on him.

Audra smiles brightly from ear-to-ear, completely elated to see him.

"Mister Zachary! It's so good of you to drop in like this." She laughs. "Please, allow me to introduce my sister, Arriana."

Rye Michaels walks into the South Star plaza entrance and is met by Roger Dane and security guards.

Roger looks at him. "You don't really expect me to make any deals."

"I expect you to be a man of your word." Rye tells him.

"I only made promises to get you to return." Roger says.

Rye smiles. "I've returned. Now let's talk business."

Roger hesitates momentarily then relents. "Very well. Come to my office."

The security guards escort Rye and they all follow Roger.

Rye was surprised to hear about Frank and Tony, but then again, he wasn't all that surprised, knowing Frank the way he did. So now he has to change his plans to make certain they can't go back.

In Roger's office, Rey sees a photograph on the wall of Doctor Jackson Kaiden Ashly.

Audra and Arriana talk with Frank while security guards keep him handcuffed.

"No one hides in ventilation shafts anymore, Frank."

Audra Kids him.

"I guess I must be behind time." He says.

Arriana laughs. "That's a clever joke, mister Zachary."

"Well, you're certainly a step ahead of whoever tried to shoot you." Audra says.

Frank furrows his brow, "I've run out of steps. Do they know who did it?" He asks. He suspect Rye Michaels had something to do with it.

"Not yet, but Security is thoroughly investigating." Audra tells him.

Just then two guards bring in a very hung-over Tony Joshua.

Frank cautions everyone, "Well, until they find out whoever tried to kill us, we're still in danger."

Tony moans. The security guards move about uncomfortably and keep looking around nervously.

Roger Dane enter alone. He takes Audra aside and whispers to her. "Our computer experts have discovered something."

"Did they gain access to Frank's computer programs?" She asks.

"Partially." He tells her. "It seems that he ran a security program to block our cameras here in the laboratory."

"Then it stands to reason that he was in here running programs." She supposes.

"We still don't know who tried to kill them." Roger tells her. Then he turns to the security guards. "Take Zachary and Joshua to our Debriefing Room and guard them well."

"If y' all don't mind," Arriana says, "I'd like to accompany mister Zachary and mister Joshua. There are a few things I would like to discuss with them.

Roger hesitates at first, but since she's the wife of a Senator, he agrees and the guards escort all of them out of the laboratory.

In the debriefing room, Arriana takes a closer look at their clothes. "My word! Look at these nasty clothes." She exclaims. "We certainly have much better outfits than this. We have the very latest fashion designs."

She turns to the guards and blurts out in a highly exaggerated Confederate accent: "Y'all go get me two pair of those delicious looking chocolate brown coveralls. Right now! Go, go, go!"

Frank smiles and rubs his chin, occasionally shaking his head. He's never seen Arriana this way before and he's not sure he likes it.

A guard scurries out at her command. The wife of a prominent Senator is no one to argue with. Arriana turns back to Frank and Tony.

"Now then, Gentlemen, I wish to thank you both very, very much for what you are doing for my sister, Audra. I don't really believe that you are time travelers, but then whoever you are, this fabulous trick of yours has saved her little program. It just broke her heart when they shut it down. So, if there is anything at all I can do for you, please just let me know... And I do mean anything at all!"

Frank just smiles, but Tony has other ideas. He takes full advantage of her offer and plays the part to the fullest. "Actually, our part in this is over, so we'd just like to go back home." Tony tells her. "We live in Denver and we'd appreciate a ride."

Arriana nods. "Y'all stay right here. I'll be back shortly with a limousine."

Tony smiles. Frank scratches his head like 'why didn't I think of that?' as Arriana hurries out.

In Roger Dane's office, Rye is sitting at Dane's desk when Roger returns. He's holding the photo of Jackson Kaiden Ashley in his lap.

Roger tells him, "We need to know how to access Frank Zachary's computer programs."

"I don't know his access codes." Rye says.

"Then tell us as much as you know and we'll figure the rest out for ourselves."

Rye balks. "Not unless we reach an understanding... Oh, by the way..." Rye holds up the photograph. "What happened to Doctor Jackson Kaiden Ashley?"

Roger trembles a little, then "Ah, there was an accident..." he hesitates.

"Accident?" Rye queries.

"Yes. He's in a sort of a Rest Home." Roger tells him.

"He's alive?" Rye wants to know more now.

"Yes. They're taking good care of him. It's a kind of Nursing Home."

Rye sees another opportunity. Maybe he can offer to help Audra time travel back and prevent Jackson's 'accident'.

Roger's phone rings and he answers it. They want Roger back in the Laboratory right away. After he hangs up he turns back to Rye. "We'll discuss that understanding when I return."

"Hurry back." Rye tells him.

In the Laboratory, Audra looks over the shoulder of a computer Operator who types rapidly then sits back with a big smile on his face. Audra pats the Operator on the back.

"As soon as Roger arrives we'll activate it." She tells him.

Roger enters and Audra excitedly waves at him. He comes to the Control Panel and Audra reaches over and punches a key on the computer and Frank's system goes on. The large accelerators activate and the wormhole appears on the central platform. Then the small negative accelerator overhead turns on and the wormhole stabilizes.

"Excellent!" Roger exclaims. "This must be Frank's program."

"Yes. Your computer expert accessed it. We believe this is his Prehistoric program." Audra says excitedly. "I changed the time setting to daylight hours... around noon."

"Let's send a mobile communicator with a camera to check it out," Roger says.

He waves and the Technicians carry over a small portable machine on wheels with a camera mounted on it and set it in front of the wormhole.

From the control panel, they operate the mobile unit by remote control and send it into the wormhole. Then everyone looks at a large screen on the wall and they turn on the camera.

They see the Prehistoric Plateau on the screen. They

move the mobile unit out farther and swivel the camera to pan the area.

Roger turns to the Technicians again. "Bring in their recorders and camcorders and let's make a comparison. This scene looks familiar."

The Technicians bring in Rye's Monitoring recorders and Tony's cameras. They begin replaying them to compare with the scenery being projected on the large screen from their mobile communicator on the plateau.

"Yes. This looks much the same." Audra comments.

They all move up to the screen for a closer look.

Roger asks, "Did he already go there? If so, what did he do? Perhaps he was just planning to go there later. Wait!" He suddenly exclaims, as he sees something out of order.
"Do that again! Move the camera back to that rock!" he orders the Technicians.

They swivel the camera to pan back to the sundial rock and stop it there.

Audra says, "Now re-run their video camcorder."
They re-run the camcorder of the sundial rock and Roger points to their own screen that shows the tree branch that Frank and Tony tied to the rock.

"There!" Roger exclaims. "I see it. There's a large stick of some kind tied against that rock. It's not there in these videos. Frank must have put it there so that Tony would not fall off and change things." He moves away from the screen. "We must remove it at once. Call Jones! Also bring Frank and Tony back in here."

Once again the Laboratory becomes a beehive as they make preparations.

Frank and Tony are putting on their new chocolate brown coveralls that Arriana ordered for them when the guards enter and escort them out.

"Hey! Wait until I get these things zipped up! Jeez!" Tony exclaims.

The guards hustle them out. When they enter the Laboratory, they see that the wormhole is active. Frank looks at the large screen and immediately knows what he sees. He cringes. The guards handcuff Frank and Tony to a post.

"Please make yourselves comfortable." Roger tells them. "We're about to begin. I'm certain that this will interest you." he says to Frank.

Jones enters. He is hermetically sealed in an outfit and wearing an oxygen mask with an oxygen tank on his back. He moves to the central platform. Roger gives him a photograph.

"This photograph shows where that tree branch was before they put it on the rock. Go put it back." Jones nods and heads for the wormhole.

Arriana enters and looks around. "They told me that my passengers were here... Oh my goodness!" She says when she sees Frank and Tony handcuffed and then she sees the scene on the big screen. She goes and stands next to Audra.

Jones steps into the wormhole and disappears. Soon he appears on the big screen on the Laboratory wall walking toward the sundial rock holding up the photograph. Frank cringes again and looks away. "Will this screw us up?" Tony asks him.

"Don't worry about it." Frank tells him. "We'll figure something out.

Roger observes Frank closely. He turns to Audra, "I

want to see how Mister Zachary reacts to all this." Audra says nothing and just looks sadly at Frank.

On the screen they see Jones remove the tree branch and put it back where it was. Then he returns to the mobile camera, walks past it and he soon exits the wormhole onto the central platform in the South Star Laboratory. Everyone cheers. They bring the mobile communicator back in and shut down the program.

As the wormhole fades away and the accelerators wind down, Roger walks over and takes a closer look at Frank. Frank raises his head and a slight sly smile begins to spread across his face. Tony scratches his head. Roger looks concerned now that Frank is smiling. Frank is bluffing, of course.

"Thank you, Doctor Dane. You just solved our problem for us." Frank blurts out as he grins broadly.

Tony is puzzled. Roger becomes very disturbed and turns to Audra.

"Save that Program! I'll get to the bottom of this. Guards! Bring both of them to my office." Roger commands as he storms out of the Laboratory.

Arriana looks at the screen then turns to Audra. "This all looks real nice, Audra. I don't have any idea what it's all about, but it does look real nice. Y'all come visit sometime. Bye now."

Audra smiles at her sister as Arriana exits. The guards escort Frank and Tony out of the Laboratory.

The guards escort Frank and Tony into Roger Dane's office while Roger is on the telephone. Roger is alone and he hangs up the phone. "Just how did we solve your problem?" He asks Frank.

Frank remains silent. Tony is still puzzled. Roger looks to Tony for an answer.

Tony shrugs his shoulders, "Don't look at me." he says.

Roger sees that Frank won't talk so he turns to the guards, "Very well, take them to the new detention area and guard them well."

The guards escort Frank and Tony out.

After they've gone, Rye Michaels comes in from the next room.

"Well, whatever trap he set up on the Prehistoric Plateau, you'll never get it out of him now." Rye tells Roger.

"That's what you're going to tell us." Dane advises him.

As the four security guards lead Frank and Tony down the hallway toward the new detention area, Frank acts like he trips then turns on them using his karate. Tony attacks the others using his karate and they both knock out the guards. Frank gets the handcuff keys from the pocket of one of the guards and unlocks their cuffs. He and Tony go to the supply room where they have more items stashed, then they head back down the hall and wait to make certain no one is in the Laboratory.

As soon as they are sure the Lab is clear, they enter and move to the central platform with their gear. Frank moves quickly to the control panel and activates his programs then runs over and retrieves the detonator he stashed under the console when he fell from the ventilator shaft.

The accelerators come to life and the wormhole appears. He clicks a handheld activator and the vortex stabilizes.

In a panic, Roger, Rye Michaels, and Security Guards rush into the Laboratory and charge toward them just as Frank and Tony are moving into the wormhole.

Rye screams, "Don't let them go! They'll destroy South Star!" Rye pulls out and fires a pistol and hits Tony in the arm.

Frank grabs Tony and pulls him into the wormhole.

A Security Guard grabs the pistol from Rye's hand.

Rye dives through the vortex just as Frank pushes the button on the remote control detonator that sets off the explosives with a loud boom and damages the Small Negative Accelerator.

The wormhole becomes unstable right after Frank, Tony and Rye are gone.

The Guards start to follow them into the wormhole, but Roger yells at them to stop.

"Don't try to follow them! The wormhole is no longer stable. Stay away from it! You may get lost in time like the others!"

The Guards stop abruptly.
Audra enters and they shut down the accelerators.
They all stare at the vortex as it disappears and wonder what will happen to them next.

On the Prehistoric Plateau, we see a repeat of Tony Joshua of TX-7 in khaki coveralls screaming in panic as he dives headlong into the diminishing wormhole to South Star. Tony disappears into the vortex then the wormhole flickers and fades out.

Moments later the wormhole reappears with more stability and much brighter. Frank and injured Tony exit this wormhole wearing the chocolate brown coveralls they received in South Star. Frank helps Tony out of the wormhole and Rye Michaels comes flying through just before the vortex suddenly disappears, because Frank sabotaged the small accelerator. At this time, none of them realize that they have returned to the Prehistoric Plateau <u>after</u> their trip to South Star, and that they have just missed bumping into themselves.

When the vortex stops Rye yells at Frank, "Dammit, Frank! Now we can't go back."

It's raining harder than Frank expected so he checks his chronometer.

"Oh no! He exclaims. "This time we came back too late!"

Rye gets up, charges and tackles Frank and Tony and all three go sprawling in the mud. Rye and Frank fight furiously while Tony picks himself up out of the mud holding his injured arm. Tony moves to try and stop them then changes his mind and just stands and watches.

Lightning flashes and thunderclaps and the storm and rains increase in intensity.

As Tony watches them fight, he notices a reflection against the sheet of rainfall in front of him. He turns around and sees a light. He squints for a better look, moves closer and sees another vortex. Excitedly Tony yells and screams at them:

"Wormhole! Hey, you guys! <u>WORMHOLE!!!</u>

Frank and Rye stop fighting when they hear Tony shout. They move closer and see the wormhole themselves. Rye gets excited. "Yes! South Star is back! Hah!"

Rye runs and dives headlong into the vortex and disappears.

Frank and Tony stand in the rain and stare at the

wormhole.

"I wonder what they'll do to us this time." Tony says.

"Your guess is as good as mine." Frank responds.

Frank turns and looks at the sundial rock. "Maybe this time we can reinforce that pointed rock you overturned so they won't notice."

"Hey, yeah. Then when I grab it, it won't turn over." Tony comments. That would solve their problem right there. If the cockroaches don't get loose and they don't kill any of them, then they won't change history.

Suddenly several heavily armed Security Guards wearing rain gear exit the wormhole. They move slowly toward Frank and Tony with weapons aimed at them. The Guards motion toward the wormhole and escort Frank and Tony into it.

Frank, Tony and the Security Guards exit the wormhole onto the central platform in the Laboratory. Rye is handcuffed and being held down by two other guards. Frank looks around and sees a more familiar setting.

The sign overhead reads, "PROJECT TX-7". The calendar reads, "November, 2000." The clock on the wall reads "5 p.m." They are back home exactly two hours after they left.

Rye screams at Frank. "You bastard, Frank! You destroyed South Star! We're right back where we started!"

Audra and Roger, looking the same as when the Time Team first left, approach them.

"Frank, are you alright?" Roger asks.

Frank shakes his head and turns to Tony smiling. "We're <u>HOME</u>, Tony!"

"How did that happen?" Tony asks him.

"I don't know." Frank answers.

Frank yells. "Medic! Medic! Tony needs medical attention right away!"

The Medics come over and tend to Tony's wounded arm.

Audra asks Frank. "What happened to Ryan Michael's <u>coveralls</u>?"

Frank and Tony are covered with mud from head to foot so that no one notices the color or shape of their coveralls.

"They must have been torn when the lightning struck so close to us." Frank says, trying not to reveal anything too soon until they can figure out what happened.

Roger orders, "Take Ryan and Tony to the Infirmary immediately."

As the Medics take Rye and Tony out, Frank moves away from the central platform and approaches Audra. He shakes his head back and forth indicating to her that his mission to go back and prevent Patty's death failed.

Everyone looks questioning at Frank. He hands the bag containing their equipment and recorder/camera to the Technicians.

"Everything is recorded here." Frank says. "This should answer all your questions."

The Technicians open the bag and take out the recorders and begin to examine them as Frank heads for the door.

Arriana enters...HIS Arriana. Frank rushes over and throws his arms around her giving her big hugs and kisses. "Boy am I glad to see you!"

She hugs him back. "I'm just glad you made it back okay."

Then he looks at her sadly and reassures her. "Don't worry, we'll try again soon."

Audra comes and asks Frank. "Ryan Michaels was ranting and raving about a 'South Star'. What was that all about?"

Frank responds cautiously. "That was the result of a paradox. I'll explain it all in my report and answer any necessary questions later."

Then Audra explains, "Rye said you were all in South Star for two days. You've only been gone from here for <u>two hours</u>."

Frank checks his chronometer with the clock on the wall. "Yes, I noticed that. We've been gone two hours." Then he begs off, "I'm a mess. I'd better go get cleaned up."

"Very well." says Roger. "Then meet us in the Debriefing Room."

Frank nods as he and Arriana head for the showers. Later that night in the TX-7 Debriefing Room, Roger and Audra discuss the great mystery, as the Technicians set up Rye's monitor recordings and Tony's camcorders.

"I don't understand their ravings about it." She says.

"Maybe Frank can explain it when he gets here." Roger tells her. "Maybe the lightning."

The Technicians begin testing the recordings and projecting them on two large wall screens. Audra instructs them, "Run them all fast forward until we get to the part when that lightning struck the wormhole."

Roger agrees with her, "Yes, we know how it

affected us here, but what we don't know is what happened on the Prehistoric Plateau."

They run them fast forward to the part where the lightning flashes all around the time travelers. They see Frank, Tony and Rye dive for cover. The lightning hits the wormhole. From that point on the recordings are confused, overlapped and double exposed. The images are very strange, because they think they can even see themselves differently dressed and in unusual, or elaborate settings.

"All right." says Audra. "That lightning strike hit the wormhole about two hours before the team came back in. Then Rye Michaels came diving in and didn't realize where he was."

"He must have been delirious from being struck by the lightning." Roger says.

Frank and Arriana enter. Frank is clean now and dressed in street clothes. He goes immediately to look at the projections on the screens. "Run them back again, please." Frank requests. They rerun all the recordings. Frank is puzzled and shakes his head.

"We're hoping you can explain what happened." Roger tells him.

Frank doesn't respond. He just keeps studying the projections.

Then Audra informs him, "At four-fifty-two p.m. there was a tremendous power surge when the lightning struck the wormhole, but our lightning arresters grounded it."

Frank turns toward Audra and listens to her with great interest.

She continues, "Then immediately following the lightning strikes, there was a tremendous power drain, and our back-up generators and accelerators came on-line to compensate."

Frank listens with even greater interest now as she continues, "The power drain lasted for only a few minutes then everything went back to normal, and the back-up generators and accelerators shut down."

Frank furrows his brow, "First the power surge...then the power drain," he muses.

"At first I thought you..." Audra catches herself. She thought Frank activated the second wormhole to rescue Patty. Then she quickly changes the subject. "Uh... We visited Ryan and Tony at the Infirmary and..."

Roger continues for her, "Both of them must have been out of their minds. What a strange tale they had to tell. But now nothing in these recordings can back up their claims about any South Star. Ryan claims that they stopped recording when their gear was confiscated. It sounded more like one of those alien abduction stories." Both recordings show Frank, Rye and Tony diving for cover when the lightning flashes all around them. Then they are scurrying toward the wormhole afterward. There is very little recorded after that. Frank remains silent and continues studying the recordings closely.

Audra conjectures, "It seems highly unlikely that they would both have the same hallucinations. And then there is the question of Tony's very unusual looking coveralls that he insisted on keeping. He said he might start a new fad with them."

"What is your story about this South Star, Frank?" Roger asks.

Frank continues to study the recordings as he responds. "I'm afraid I don't have one. I guess Rye and Tony were hit by the same bolt of lightning."

Audra decides that she's had enough. "It will take some time for our Specialists to clear up these recordings. I'm returning to my office. Call me when they're ready."
As she leaves, she motions to Frank that she wants to see him.

Roger tells Frank, "I know you well enough to know you're not going to say anything, until we start asking specific questions about these recordings... if and when we ever get them cleared up."

"I'll check back with you then." Frank says as he and Arriana follow Audra.

Rye Michaels is laying on an Infirmary bed in restraints while Tony is looking out the window. `Be it ever so humble..." Tony says. Rye tugs at his restraints. "Tell me what happened, Joshua."

"I don't know what happened. Frank doesn't even know what happened. I don't really care. We're back home." Tony tells him.

"This is crap compared to that perfect world of South Star and you know it." Rye says.

Tony laughs and turns to face him as he says, "That's okay. I couldn't live in such a perfect world. I'm too used to a life of chaos."

Audra is pacing back and forth in her office when Frank and Arriana enter. Frank reaches into his pocket and pulls out her special activator. He points to the burn marks.

"Lightning strike. It blew the fuses before I could travel back. Those South Star people repaired it." he tells her.

Arriana looks at him, "Now, just what the heck is this South Star thing?"

"I'll explain it all later. Right now I'm only interested in one thing...going back to save Patty. Okay?" he says.

Audra takes the activator and opens it. She looks at it very closely. "My word! Look at these fuses and the computer chips. Absolutely fantastic! They're years ahead of us."

Frank shakes his head. "All I want to know is if it still works and how long it will take to get set up for another try."

I'll have to run some tests on it in the Laboratory." Audra says as she puts it in her pocket and heads for the door with Frank and Arriana right behind her.

In the Laboratory, Audra, Frank and Arriana move to a more isolated workbench area where Audra tests the special activator. Then she closes it and hands it to Frank.

"I think this will work even better than before," she tells him.

"I want to go directly to the Synergist Building from here," he says.

Audra stringently objects. "We can't do that. The program is already set up. If we change it now they'll know. The Committee will terminate all of us and then they'll change it to the way it was."

Arriana adds, "You must go to the Prehistoric Plateau first, and from that point back to the alley behind the Synergist Building."

"Yes. Just like we planned before. Only this time you'll go back to prehistory two and one-half hours later, so you won't bump into yourself." Audra explains.

Arriana starts getting upset. "The storm will still be in progress to power the second wormhole, but you won't have as much time because the storm will end sooner."

Frank reassures her. "I'll just have to move faster."

Later that night, Frank slips into the Laboratory wearing black coveralls and a utility belt with weapons as well as tools. He sneaks in and locks all the doors just as he did in the South Star Laboratory. Then he moves fast to the control panel, turns on the computer and begins typing.

He proceeds quickly to the central platform where he puts on heavy rain boots, a full-length raincoat and a rain hat. He takes out the standard activator and clicks it. The large accelerators become active and the wormhole appears. He clicks it again for the small accelerator and the vortex stabilizes. He checks to make sure he has his Special Activator then he moves toward the central platform.

Rye Michaels had escaped from the Infirmary. He had his own lock picking devices. He arrived at the Laboratory while Frank was activating the wormhole.

In the world of South Star, Doctor Audra Ashley had made a duplicate of Frank's Special Activator. Rye had pocketed it before they returned to TX-7. He checks his pocket to make sure he still has it. He sees how Frank is dressed and he leaves to change his clothes.

Frank steps into the wormhole and disappears.

On the Prehistoric Plateau, five million years ago, Frank exits the wormhole into the storm. The torrential rain makes it hard to see. Lightning flashes and thunder claps as Frank moves away from the first wormhole.

He takes out Audra's special activator, clicks it and activates the second wormhole. There is lightning and thunder again, but this time the second wormhole remains stable.

Frank waits a moment to make sure it stays stable then steps into the second wormhole.

Rye Michaels returns to the Laboratory now dressed in black coveralls like Frank. He also has a utility belt with weapons. The wormhole is still active. He checks to make sure he has his Special Activator then he moves to the central platform and steps into the vortex.

Frank steps out of the second wormhole into the alley behind the Synergist Syndicate building and looks around. The weather is clear. He checks his chronometer with the Bank clock down the street for the time and date. It is May, 2000. Frank nods, satisfied that it's the right time and place.

He takes off his rain gear and stashes it behind a dumpster then starts for the back door, but he begins to get dizzy. He digs into his belt and pulls out a package marked "Doppelganger Medication". He takes out several pills and swallows them with drinking water from the canteen on his utility belt then he sits down for a moment until he feels better. He gets up and enters the back door of the Synergist building.

Rye steps out of the wormhole onto the Plateau into the storm. The thunder and lightning startle him at first. He takes out the Activator and clicks it. The second wormhole appears. He wonders about it, but then he shrugs his shoulders, moves with caution and steps into it.

Inside the Synergist Building, Frank goes to the stairwell, takes out a black hood with eyeholes in it and pulls it over his head. He screws a silencer onto the barrel of an automatic weapon and checks to make sure it's fully loaded. He pulls out a piece of paper with maps and diagrams on it, studies it briefly, then runs up the stairs taking them two and three at a time. Each floor has numbered doors and when he reaches the floor he wants, he stops and enters the hall.

Rye Michaels steps out of the second wormhole into the alley. He's not sure where he is at first, but after looking around he recognizes the Synergist Building and sees the back door. Now he understands where Frank is headed. He also becomes very dizzy, because Rye Michaels, his counterpart, is in the Banquet Room upstairs. He takes out the "Doppelganger Medication" pills and stuffs several in his mouth. He leans against the building until he feels more stable, and then goes in the back door.

Frank runs fast down the hall until he comes to a corner. He peeks around it, and sees two terrorists dressed in camouflage uniforms coming out of the Security Office. Behind them are three security guards lying on the floor.

As the two terrorists hurry down the hall they hear a noise from a door. They turn and aim their weapons at it, but see a small knife stuck in the doorframe. Quickly they both spin around only to come face-to-face with Frank, who is now standing in the middle of the hallway. Frank shoots both of them before they can move again. He walks over and pulls the small knife from the doorframe and puts it in his belt, then he runs to a window marked "Fire Escape" and crawls out. Frank climbs the fire escape stairs three at a time. At one turn, he comes to an abrupt stop when a strap from his belt catches on a handrail. He frantically yanks on it then stops, takes a deep breath and calmly reaches down to free it. He runs up the fire escape stairs to a window and tries to open it. It's locked. He breaks the window, unlocks and opens it, then climbs in and runs down the hall.

Rye must stay away from the Banquet Room, because he'll be too close to himself. He knows that's where Frank is headed. His only thought now is to kill Walt Marcson before he can talk. But how can he? He has to take the chance, so he heads for the Banquet Room anyway.

Frank will be concentrating on protecting Patty and Arriana. He also knows that Marcson heads out a side door after he shoots the Senator. Rye heads for that side door. He'll wait until Walt comes out then shoot him.

Frank is in the Banquet Room hallway now. He moves down the hall until he comes to another corner. He peeks around it and sees two more terrorists standing in front of the Banquet Room door. One of the men has a communicator to his ear, listening. Frank takes a deep breath and readies his weapon. He pulls the knife from his belt and throws it. It hits the door in front of the terrorists and both turn around and fire. He shoots both of them, but one of their bullets grazes Frank's arm. After he makes sure they're both dead, he stuffs a handkerchief in his coat-sleeve to stop the bleeding. Then he takes their communicator, takes their place at the door, listens and waits.

Inside the Banquet Room, Arriana is at the table talking with Patty. Nathan signs autographs and Tony's brother, Samurai Sam, converses with Nathan's bodyguard. Patty excitedly shows her mother all her autographs then Arriana starts back.

SUDDENLY... two masked men in camouflage uniforms charge in and shoot at the guests. Everyone dives for cover. Those two caterers pull weapons and join the attackers. Rye and Walt Marcson rush over and push Arriana under a table.

Sam and Nathan's bodyguard push Patty and Nathan under a table.

Then a second door opens and in charges Frank Zachary. The two aggressors and the two caterers look toward a third door, but it never opens. Frank shoots the two caterers. The other two Terrorists continue shooting at the guests. Sam and Nathan's bodyguard get up and fight back. They attack the two remaining Terrorists and put up a good fight. Frank looks toward the table with Arriana, Rye and Walt. Walt pulls out a pistol and aims it at the Senator. Frank shoots first. As Walt falls, his gun goes off, but it only hits the Senator in the leg this time. Then Marcson runs for that side door.

Frank turns back to the other two terrorists who are just about ready to shoot Sam and he shoots both terrorists before they can fire. No one shoots at Patty this time. No terrorists are left.

Then Frank runs quickly out of the room and down the hall.

Arriana runs over to Patty and they throw their arms around each other.

Frank comes flying out the door of the building into the alley and dashes over to the dumpster. He reaches for his rain gear, but it's all gone. He searches all around then looks up and down the alley. At the end of the alley he sees an old scrounger pushing a shopping cart full of junk items. He's wearing Frank's raincoat, hat and boots. Frank starts to go after him then he stops and decides to let it go.

Frank uses the activator and re-activates the second wormhole in the alley. He starts to enter when Rye Michaels, dressed in black and holding a weapon, comes flying out of the Synergist Building back door and yells at him.

"Oh no you don't, Frank! You're not going anywhere until this thing gets cleared up!"

Rye gets dizzy again and starts to stagger. When he reaches for more Doppelganger pills, Frank takes advantage of this and shoots first, hitting Rye in the arm, causing him to drop his weapon. While Rye is off balance, Frank attacks and they fight in the alley, but Rye is still too dizzy to put up much of a fight, so Frank just grabs him and drags him into the wormhole.

Frank comes out of the wormhole dragging Rye into the raging storm on the Prehistoric Plateau and drops Rye into a puddle of mud.

Frank had seen Walt Marcson laying dead in the hallway, so he knew someone else was involved, and he immediately suspected that it was Rye.

Rye picks himself up and staggers around a little.

"How do you feel now?" Frank asks him.

Rye is still a little dizzy as he straightens himself up. "A little better."

Frank de-activates the second wormhole and says, "I'm glad you're feeling better." Then he turns and hits Rye in the mouth with his fist and knocks him back down. "How in the hell did you get here?" Frank asks him.

Rye holds up his own Special Activator. "Doctor Audra Ashley of South Star made a duplicate of the one you have. I sort of filched it when no one was looking."

Frank shakes his head and walks toward the first wormhole, but Rye jumps up and grabs him and they fight again. "You destroyed South Star." Rye yells.

Both are wounded and they wear each other down fast. They find themselves at the edge of the plateau leaning against that sundial-shaped rock that Tony fell off. They take a breather and nurse their wounds.

Curious, they both look down at the pointed rock that Tony tipped over. Now the giant sloth they saw before has been joined by three more of his kind. All of them are tipping over rocks systematically and gobbling up the roaches. One sloth tips over the rocks on either side of the rock Tony tipped over and cockroaches pour out just like before.

Frank and Rye move closer to the edge to watch and study the situation. Frank begins to add things up. "Say! This would have happened anyway. It's a natural occurrence. Those giant sloth's would have killed all those cockroaches without Tony's help. Tony didn't make any difference...<u>Tony</u> <u>didn't change history!</u>"

"Wait a minute!" Rye exclaims. "If Tony didn't change history, then what happened?"
Frank looks up at the lightning flashes. He studies the wormhole and the lightning. "It must have been the electrical storm that did it. That's what Audra was trying to figure out. The lightning struck our wormhole and activated a second wormhole to South Star." he tells Rye.

Frank examines the wormhole from different sides. Then he thinks back to when he, Rye and Tony, dressed in khaki coveralls, were running toward the wormhole and the lightning struck, making them all dive for cover. The lightning strikes the wormhole, creating a double-wormhole, one in front of the other. The three of them unwittingly run for the <u>"ROGUE   WORMHOLE"</u> in front of the TX-7 vortex.

Frank needs to check their computers to be certain.

"Now wait a minute." Rye says. "You're saying that the lightning struck our wormhole and activated a second one."

"It's just a theory." Frank tells him. " We'll have to go back and check our computers and recorders to find out for sure."

"Then we can go back to South Star?" Rye asks.

"I don't know, but the computer does. If we return to the TX-7 Laboratory now we can determine the exact time that the lightning struck our vortex, and you can go back to South Star on your own, if you want."

Rye stares at him seriously to determine if Frank is telling the truth.

"Is that a promise?" Rye asks.

"That's a promise." Frank assures him.

Suddenly their wormhole begins to light up. It starts growing brighter and brighter then dimmer and dimmer almost like a star going Nova. Waves of light pour out of the vortex. Frank and Rye fall to the ground holding their heads.

"What's happening?" Rye asks.

"Paradox... because we stopped the attack at the Synergist Building. It changed things. We're just now feeling the effects. Hang on!" Frank tells him.

Both lay on the ground holding their heads until the paradox subsides and the waves of light fade away and the wormhole stabilizes again.

Rye leans up on his elbows and starts laughing as their memories begin to change.

"I recollect things differently now. They figured that Walt Marcson not only arranged the attack and the kidnapping, but also had a personal grudge against Senator Genna." Rye says.

"Then Senator Genna got the TX-7 Monitor contracts back for Synergist." Frank adds.

"Yeah, dammit! I wanted to get some credit for that."

Rye says. "Oh Well..."

Frank picks himself up out of the mud and gives Rye a hand up.

"Things haven't changed that much, Franklin. I still remember South Star." Rye says.

"I remember South Star, too. But you're wrong about nothing being different. Patty and Samurai Sam are alive now." Frank tells him.

"Are you sure about that?" Rye asks.

"Let's go back and find out." Frank says.

They both step into the TX-7 wormhole and disappear.

Frank and Rye come out of the wormhole into the TX-7 Laboratory. Both are soaking wet and covered with mud. Frank pulls out the standard activator and shuts it all down. They both examine the laboratory to make sure they're in the right time and place. Frank picks up the telephone and dials home.

Patty Zachary runs over and answers the telephone at the Zachary residence.

"Hello...daddy! Where are you?" She turns and yells to her mother. "Mom, it's dad!" Patty squeals. Arriana stops at the doorway, holding a dishtowel, smiling. She throws the towel over her shoulder, raises her voice so Frank can hear her over the phone. "What time is he coming home?" Arri yells.

"He says he has to clean up a little bit of a mess then he'll be right home." Patty answers.

Arriana yells again, "Ask him what kind of trouble

they had on the test."

"Daddy, they told us you guys had some trouble. Will you tell us all about it when you get home? Please!" Patty pleads. "Something about a South Star. Tell us, please, please...
Okay...I love you. Bye." Patty hangs up the phone.

At the TX-7 Laboratory, Frank hangs up the phone with a big smile on his face and tears in his eyes. Then he picks up the phone and dials another number.

"Who y'all calling now?" Rye asks.

I'm calling the Infirmary to check on Tony...if he's still with us. I don't know what all that paradox caused." Frank informs him.

In the Infirmary, Tony, lying on the bed with his arm bandaged, reaches over and picks up the phone. "Hello... Hey, Frank, my mom and my brother Sam came to visit me."

Sam and their mother are standing next to Tony's bed. Both are smiling.

"Sam feels bad because he talked me into taking this job." Tony tells him. "But I wouldn't have missed out on this for anything in the world. Bye." Tony hangs up.

Frank hangs up the phone with a big smile on his face and takes a deep breath. "Tony has visitors ... His mother and his brother Samurai Sam. Mission accomplished!"

Rye tells him, "For you, maybe. But I still remember things differently."

"So do I now." Frank says.

"I'm talking about South Star. I still think you destroyed it when everything changed back. I'll never forgive you for destroying South Star." Rye moans.

Frank yells at him at the top of his lungs. "I DID <u>NOT</u> DESTROY SOUTH STAR!!!"

Then he glares at Rye and speaks slowly with emphases and more deliberately.

"I... Did NOT...Destroy...South...Star!"

In the <u>Parallel World </u>of SOUTH STAR, Doctor Audra Ashley stands at the base of two ladders in the South Star Laboratory. The Technicians are trying to repair the damaged Small Negative Accelerator that was sabotaged by Frank as he and Tony escaped through the wormhole, back to the prehistoric plateau and their world of TX-7.

"Don't move it! Whatever you do, do not move it!" she tells them.

The Technicians are startled when she yells at them and one of them drops a tool.

"I'm sorry, Doctor Ashley." The Tech says. "It's very difficult to work on it up here. It would help if we just brought it down."

"No. It must not be moved." Audra insists. "It must remain exactly where it is. That position is vital. Just be careful."

Doctor Roger Dane enters escorting a very distinguished looking Frank Zachary.

This Frank Zachary wears spectacles, a very stylish

three-piece suit and tie, and is sporting a well-trimmed goatee.

"Audra, allow me to introduce Doctor Franklin Joseph Zachary, Professor of Physics at M. I. T." Roger says.

Audra spins around and gets very excited. "Oh my word! We do have our own Frank Zachary! How marvelous!" she exclaims. She rushes over and very enthusiastically shakes his hand. "I am so very happy to meet you, Doctor Zachary."

Franklin Zachary is somewhat amused as well as taken aback. "Likewise, Doctor Ashley." Franklin says. He looks around the Laboratory scrutinizing everything.

Roger tells him, "This is what I was telling you about, Doctor."

Franklin shakes his head. "So, you really are experimenting with time travel."

Roger continues, "Please look around all you wish. As I explained on our way here, we desperately need your help."

Audra hands Franklin a copy of Frank Zachary's TX-7 Operations Manual.

"We had a visitor and he left us a little memento," she tells Franklin. "I'm sure you'll find it very interesting, Doctor."

Franklin skims through the manual. He sees Frank's name in it along with Audra's and Dane's and then he begins to read it more enthusiastically. Soon, he becomes totally engrossed in it. He checks Frank's Manual against the surrounding laboratory equipment. "This is absolutely fascinating!" he exclaims.

The two Technicians working on the small

accelerator on the ladders see Franklin Zachary and become very nervous. "Omigod!" says one. "How did that evil Doctor Zachary get in here? They went to such great lengths to keep him from finding out about this project."

"I don't know." The other says. "But act like you don't know who he is, or we may end up lost in time like the others."

Franklin walks to the central platform and looks around. He examines the larger accelerators then he looks up at the small accelerator being repaired. The Technicians become even more nervous and drop another tool or two.

Roger Dane comes over to Franklin and asks, "Excuse me, Doctor Zachary. Do you know anything about Parallel Universe Theory?"

"Parallel Universe, or Parallel World?" Franklin asks him back. "There's quite a difference, you know."

Roger asks, "How so?"

"A Parallel Universe is very much different from our universe in almost every aspect," Franklin tells him. "Whereas, "<u>A Parallel World</u>" is exactly like our world, except that it may have an alternate, or different history." Franklin explains.

"I believe our visitors came from a Parallel World." Audra concludes.

"Yes." Roger says. "Frank Zachary looked quite a bit like you."

Franklin raises his eyebrows at this remark. Roger tries to correct himself. "Er...but, not nearly as well dressed, nor as well groomed...nor...uh..."

"Oh dear! Look at the time!" Audra exclaims as she looks at the clock on the wall.

It is 11:45 p.m. on November 7th in the year 2000. It's <u>Election Day!</u>

"I wonder who won the Presidential Election," she ponders.

Franklin looks up from the manual and responds. "George W. Bush."

Roger blurts out in surprise. "That Texas Republican!"

Then Audra exclaims in her finest Confederate accent.

"My word! What will this country come to now!"

In the TX-7 Laboratory of our world, Frank and Rye are changing into clean dry clothes.

Rye asks, "If South Star still exists in a parallel world, like you say, then how do we get back there again?"

"What do you mean <u>WE</u>?" Frank asks.

"All right." Rye responds. "How do I get back there?"

Frank thinks about it for a minute. "Let me check the computer tomorrow. I think the lightning strike and our power surge here may have activated the South Star wormhole. I'll let you know."

Rye stares at him intently. "Is that a promise?" He asks.

"Yes." Frank replies. "That's a promise."

In the automobile going home, Frank is driving while Rye sits in the front passenger seat. Their differences seem to be resolved. They ride along in silence then Frank speaks.

"I want to thank you for your help, Rye." He says.

Rye scowls. "I'm sure I don't know what y'all are talking about."

Frank smiles. "We were partners once, remember? I know you well enough, because of our old days as Training Instructors with the Navy SEALS. When you are antagonistic and hostile toward someone, it's because you're trying to help them. Whenever you're nice to someone, you're about ready to stick a knife in their ribs."

Rye doesn't say anything. He just looks out the passenger side window as Frank drives along. He shuffles in his seat a little uncomfortably.

Rye backed up Frank, but he doesn't want anyone to know about it. He doesn't like anyone to know his moves. He hoped it worked, but he still had his doubts.

"I know you were on a big guilt trip when Patty got killed." Frank tells him. "Well, she's alive now, so..."

Rye cuts him off, "Are you really sure about that?" He's still distraught over it.

"Come with me to my house and find out for yourself." Frank pleads with him.

Rye shakes his head and holds up his cell phone. "Just drop me off around the corner from your place. I'll call a taxi. Your word that you'll show me how to return to South Star."

"You have my word." Frank says as he pulls the car over to the curb. Rye gets out of the car under the corner street lamp.

As Frank drives away, Rye moves quickly into the bushes and trees on the corner and watches closely as Frank drives up to his house. Trying to get a closer look, Rye trips over a trash can and knocks it over with a bang. He swears and kicks the can then moves closer so he can see the front of Frank's house.

Frank pulls into the driveway and parks. He gets out of the car and rubs his shoulder that is now freshly bandaged. A little nervous, he walks slowly toward the door.

The front door flies open and his daughter Patty comes running out.

"Hi daddy!" she squeals throwing her arms around him and giving him a big kiss and hug, almost knocking him over. Frank winces from his shoulder wound, but doesn't let on. He kisses her, hugs her and holds her extra tight. Tears come to his eyes again and he struggles to fight back a flood of emotions.

From the corner, Rye sees Patty come running out of the house and into her father's arms. Rye drops to his knees in prayer...redeemed. "Thank God, she's alive! Thank God!"

Rye gets up off his knees and moves out of the shadows back under the street lamp. He takes out his cell phone and calls for a taxi. "South Star here I come!"

Frank is still hugging Patty when Arriana comes to the door and yells at them. "Okay, you guys! Come on in!"

Frank and Patty head for the front door and Frank gives Arriana a big hug and a kiss as well. Again he hugs and kisses both of them and they all go into the house together.

115

The End

About the Author…

Z. O. Anderson lives in the Denver Metropolitan area of Colorado. Besides the 'South Star Trilogy' that he is currently working on, he also has several other stories that he is writing, a novel, 'They Called Him Razu', plus a screenplay, 'The Temple Rock' and a short story called VICI from BICI.

SOUTH STAR

SOUTH STAR

SOUTH STAR

9 781615 000036